NIGHT AFTER NIGHT

Book #1 in the Seductive Nights series

Lauren Blakely

ALSO BY LAUREN BLAKELY
Available at all fine e-tailers

ALSO BY LAUREN BLAKELY
Available at all fine e-tailers

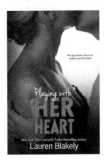

ABOUT
NIGHT AFTER NIGHT

"Let me control your pleasure."

Their world was sex, love, and lies.

He intoxicated her. Commanded. Consumed.

With a dirty mind and a mouth to match, Clay Nichols is everything Julia Bell never knew she wanted and exactly what she cannot have. He walked into her life one night and unlocked pleasure in her that she never knew was possible. Possessing her body, captivating her every thought. Which makes him way too dangerous for Julia to risk her heart, given that she has a price tag on her head. She ran after one mind-blowing week with him, but now he's back, and determined to make her his own.

No matter the cost.

She was a sexy drug to him. Fiery, unforgettable, and never enough, Julia is an enigma, and Clay isn't willing to let her go without a fight. But she's got dark secrets of her own that threaten to destroy any chance of happiness. She's a wanted woman – the stakes are high, her every move is watched, and yet the lure between them can't be denied. Can two people burned by love trust again when desire and passion are met by danger at every turn?

A sensual, emotionally-charged erotic romance from the New York Times and USA Today Bestselling author Lauren Blakely...

AUTHOR'S NOTE

Dear Readers: I am so very thrilled to share Clay and Julia's love story with you. This is a story that readers asked for! Clay and Julia originally starred in a very short story I published in late December, and countless readers asked me to write a novel for them. So I did! In fact, I wrote two novels and I expanded the short story into a novella. If you have read the original version of First Night, I encourage you to re-read the newly expanded prequel. I've included it in this ebook, and it's also available for free across all retailers. If you've read the new version of First Night skip ahead to NIGHT AFTER NIGHT to see what happens next!

ABOUT FIRST NIGHT

It was only supposed to be one night...

When the sinfully handsome man walks into her bar in San Francisco, Julia Bell simply wants a break from the troubles that keep chasing her. That escape comes in the form of sexy, confident and commanding Clay Nichols, who captivates her mind AND turns her inside out with pleasure. The attraction is electric and they share one scorchingly hot night together, but they also discover there is more than just off-the-charts chemistry; the connection between them runs deep. Clay never thought he'd return to New York with this woman still on his mind. But he can't get her out of his system, and he needs more of her...He wants more than just the first night...

CHAPTER ONE

Eight inches.

Julia longed for eight inches.

Or really, eight inches and a brain.

Was that so much for a woman to want?

Some days it seemed like it. Julia had yet to meet a man who could hold his own on all accounts, and judging from the parade of guys who seemed to think getting into a bartender's pants was as easy as ordering a drink, she wasn't sure her luck was going to change anytime soon.

Like this guy. The one with his tongue practically falling out of his mouth as he ogled her while she mixed his third Purple Snow Globe.

"Here you go," she said as she slid the sugar-rimmed martini glass to the young hipster, decked out in too tight-pants, a plaid shirt and a goatee that needed to have been shaved off.

He wiggled both eyebrows and wobbled in his chair. "And how about a phone number too?"

She flashed him her best "not a chance in hell, sucker" smile. "I've got a phone number for a taxi cab and I'd be mighty happy to provide that for you soon."

Seriously? Did he think that line was going to work? She headed to the other end of the bar to tend to a pair of blondes in low-cut halter tops, hoping they'd be less likely to hit on her. It was San Francisco though, so you never knew. But then, she was used to it. Being propositioned simply came with the territory of tending bar, and Julia Bell let all the come-on lines she heard roll off her every night, like water off a duck's back. Most of the time she barely even noticed them – they became the white noise, along with sounds of beers being poured, glasses being washed, music being played overhead at the bar she was part owner of.

Some days though, she'd like to be propositioned by a man with a brain, a witty mouth and who had the kind of body she'd want to be tied up with all night long.

Or to tie up. She was pretty sure that with the right man, she might be into some equal opportunity bondage. But he'd need to be bringing eight inches. Anything less was a deal breaker. Though, truth be told, she had little room in her life now for either eight inches or for romance. Not after the pile of problems her ex had left behind for her. A heaping mass of problems, to be precise.

She popped into the back of the bar to restock swirly straws when her phone rang. She nearly bounced as McKenna's name flashed across the screen. Julia was expecting big news from her sister tonight. After all, she'd helped McKenna's boyfriend pick out the ring.

She crossed her fingers, but then she was damn sure McKenna would say nothing but a big fat yes.

"Tell me everything," she said into the phone.

"It was amazing! He proposed to me right before the play started that his sister is in."

Julia shrieked, and wished she could wrap her sister in a big happy hug right now. "And you said yes, I hope?"

McKenna laughed. "Of course I said yes! I said yes about twenty times."

"So how did he do it?"

"Right on the frigging stage, Julia. On a Broadway stage! He proposed to me on stage!"

"Before 2000 people?"

"No, dork. Before the play started. But oh my god, I'm so happy."

Julia was grinning in the supply closet, bursting with happiness from head to toe. Her sister had been through the wringer in the romance department, but when Chris landed in her life everything changed for the better. Sunshine and roses.

McKenna shared more of the details and Julia oohed and ahhed all throughout the tale. "You better make me your maid-of-honor," she said.

"As if I'd pick anyone else."

"Good. Now that we have that settled. Are you going to get married on the beach like a proper California girl?"

"I don't know. I haven't thought that far ahead. But listen, enough about me. Chris' sister is involved with the director, and the director's buddy Clay is coming to San Fran tomorrow night for business. I told him to go to Cubic Z and say hello. I told him you were gorgeous too."

She rolled her eyes. Her sister could never resist playing the matchmaker.

"Great. But no free drinks just cause he's a friend of a friend or whatever."

"Never. But Jules," McKenna said, lowering her voice to a whisper. "The guy? Clay? He's smoking hot."

Her ears pricked. "Yeah? How smoking?"

"Un-be-lievable."

* * *

Clay Nichol's redeye to San Francisco was slated to leave in two hours, but business was business, and this deal needed to be ironclad. If he had to push the flight back, he would. He loved nothing more than negotiating and closing a deal. Fine, there was one thing he loved more than deal making. A fiery woman, the kind who could dish it out as well as she could take it. But he hadn't met anyone in the last year who excited his mind as much as his body. So for now, business was his focus. It was opening night of a new Broadway play that his friend and client, Davis Milo, had directed, and that the audience had loved. Man, that made Clay one proud entertainment lawyer since he'd sewn up the deal for Davis to direct the show, and the next one his buddy was eyeing too – a production in London.

The two men were lounging in the empty seats at the St. James Theater, chatting with the London producers.

Davis shook hands with the producers then clapped Clay on the back. "He can handle the rest. I need to go."

His friend took off, and Clay wrapped up the final details of the contract, then left the empty theater and slid into a town car. As soon as the door was closed, he loosened his purple tie; it was his good luck tie, and he always wore it on nights like these. He unbuttoned a few buttons of his crisp white shirt, stretched his neck from side to side, and reached for his phone. He hadn't been to San Francisco in a while, but he found himself googling a certain bar on the way to the airport. Who knew if he'd make it to Cubic Z, but the woman who'd been proposed to before the show had told him that her sister worked there, then added, "She's gorgeous, and the best bartender in the world."

He shrugged to himself as the car sped to La-Guardia. He wasn't sure if he'd have the time to stop by a bar in San Francisco during this trip. But he found himself wondering about the gorgeous bartender, and whether she might be the fiery type.

* * *

That had been a bitch of a deal the next day. Too many attempts at nickeling-and-diming his client – a high-profile TV talk show host in the Bay Area. Pissed him off. Clay didn't take that kind of shit and he'd made damn sure the network knew that they'd walk. That's when the exec caved and finally started playing ball. That was the secret to negotiation. Always be the one willing to walk. In the end, Clay had landed nearly every point he'd wanted for his client. But he'd felt battered and bruised with their petty ways, so he tracked down the nearest boxing gym, worked off his frustration with a long, sweaty bout with a heavy bag, pounding and punishing until his muscles screamed, and even then a little more. After, he returned to his hotel for a hot shower.

It was damn near scalding temperature as the water beat down hard on him, and he leaned into the stream, washing off the day.

When he stepped out from the water and toweled off, he was nowhere near ready to crawl into bed and call it a night. Negotiations like that warranted a drink, and as soon as the thought of a drink touched down in his head, he remembered the name of the bar, and the name of the supposedly gorgeous bartender.

Julia.

Hmmm...

He had energy to burn, and the bar wasn't far from his hotel here in the SoMa district. He pulled on jeans and a button-down shirt, combed his hair, brushed his teeth, and headed out into the San Francisco night. He only wished he'd thought to bring along a pair of handcuffs, his favorite accessory. They looked mighty fine with black lingerie, thigh-high stockings, and heels on the right woman.

But that was putting the cart before the horse, wasn't it?

CHAPTER TWO

Not Again.

Honestly, how many times was the sloppy hipster going to make a play for her? He was staring at her chest tonight. Part of her couldn't fault him. She'd been blessed in the breasts department and filled out a C-cup quite nicely, thank you very much. But still. Tact was way sexier than ogling.

"What if I ordered drinks for everyone in the bar? How about that? Would you finally give me your number then?"

"No. Because my eyes are up here," she said, and pointed to her face.

He snapped his gaze up, caught red-handed. But he was relentless. "See? I can be trained. I'm a good boy."

"I'm happy to serve you. But the number is under wraps and always will be," she told him.

The dude was practically spilled across the bar, his chest draped on the sleek metal. "How about another Appletini then?"

"No problem," she said with a private smirk. Julia loved mixing drinks – she had a bit of mad scientist in her that thrilled at discovering new combinations of flavors. But while the bartender in her enjoyed concocting a cocktail, the woman in her wished that once, just once, a guy would be a guy and order a goddamn beer. Maybe it made her shallow, but she didn't care. She would never date a man who drank the sissy drinks she often served. She liked her men to be men. No manscapers need apply.

As she mixed the hipster's drink – some vodka, some apple juice, a splash of apple brandy – a new customer sat down.

"What can I get for you?" she said before she even turned around.

"I'll take whatever's on tap."

She froze in her spot simply because the voice was rough and gravelly, and sent a charge through her with its masculine sexiness. But, the man behind that deep and husky voice was probably a dweeb, right? That'd be her luck. She plunked the Appletini down in front of her least favorite sloppy drinker, then turned to the man who wanted the beer, and holy heavenly fiesta of the eyes.

He was tall. He was broad. He had the perfect amount of stubble on his jawline, and those eyes were to-die for – deep brown and piercing. Then there was his hair – thick, brown, and ideal for sliding fingers through. She didn't want to take her eyes off him, but she knew better than to stare. She quickly straightened her spine, picked her gawking jaw up from the floor, and gave him a cool nod. "We have an India Pale Ale tonight. Will that do?"

"That'll do just fine," he said, his muscular forearms resting on the sleek bar. His shirt sleeves were rolled up and Julia couldn't help but notice how strong his arms were. She bet he worked out. A real man kind of workout. Something hard and heavy that made him sweat and grunt to mold that kind of physique. She poured the beer into the glass, and set it down in front of him. He reached for his wallet, peeled off some bills, and handed them to her.

"I take it you're Julia?"

Uh oh. How did he know her name. Was he an undercover cop? Had she accidentally served someone under twenty-one? She was diligent and methodical in her ID checking and had never let an underage in. Or wait. Her spine stiffened. Was he onto her? Did he know what she did every Tuesday night at a dimly-lit apartment above a greasy restaurant in China Town that smelled of fried pork? That would be over soon though. It had to be. She'd done her time, and was ready to cash in. Soon, she kept telling herself.

"Yeah," she answered carefully, all her senses on alert. She wasn't really doing anything wrong those nights, was she? No, she was just taking care of business as she knew how.

"I hear you're the best bartender in San Francisco."

The tightness in her shoulders relaxed. At least he wasn't a boy in blue come to bust her. But forget his smoldering looks. He was like the rest of them, going for cheap lines, hitting on the woman behind the bar. "Yeah, where'd you hear that? Facebook?"

He smiled briefly and shook his head. Damn, he had a fabulous smile. Straight, white teeth and a knowing grin. But she knew better than to fall for a hot stranger simply because he was handsome. She'd done that before, and it had kicked her in the ass. That's why she was a No-Strings-Attached kind of woman these days. Not that she'd had any attachments of any sort lately – she had too much trouble to untangle herself from before she could even think about getting tangled up in love, let alone the sheets.

"No. Your sister told me. McKenna, I believe."

Oh.

Oh yes.

It all made sense now.

And far be it from Julia to ever doubt her big sister. Because McKenna's assessment was one hundred and fifty percent correct. He was smoking hot. Un-be-liev-able. And he was no longer a stranger. He was sister-approved, he wasn't a cop, and he wasn't a heavy, so she shucked off her worries. "Clay Nichols," he said, offering a hand to shake. Nice firm grip. Before she knew it, she was thinking of other uses for those strong hands.

"Julia Bell."

"So how's your day working out for you, Julia Bell?"

She laughed once. Not because it was funny, but because it was such a simple and direct question. It wasn't a cheesy line. "It's not too shabby," she said. "And yours, Clay Nichols?"

He shook his head, let out a long stream of air. "Long, annoying, but ultimately victorious."

"What, are you a fighter?"

"Nah. Just a lawyer," he said then took a drink of the beer. He nodded to the glass in admiration. "Insert lawyer joke here."

"A lawyer walks into a bar," she said, then stopped to shoot him a playful stare. "Actually, that's not a joke. That's me giving a play by play."

He laughed. "You are an excellent commentator so far."

"Why thank you. I can keep it up all night," she said.

"All night? Is that so?" He raised an eyebrow, and his lips curved up in a wickedly sexy grin.

"It just might be. So, you were victorious. Does that mean you won your case?"

"Just won the right terms in the negotiations. My client is happy. That's what matters."

"What kind of law?" she asked, praying he wasn't going to say something seedy or sleazy – like personal injury law.

"Entertainment law," he said in that deep, rumbly voice that she was already digging.

"I'm a big fan of entertainment. Movies and me, we're like that," she said, twisting her middle and index finger together.

"Likewise. I wouldn't do it if I didn't enjoy the work. But I know what it is, and I know what it's not. I'm not saving the world. I'm not putting the bad guys behind bars. I'm just trying to help actors, directors, and TV show hosts get the best deals they can get. Put on a show, make some people happy. That's all I do."

Julia tapped the side of his beer glass. "And I believe I'm in the same field then. I'm not curing cancer. I'm not saving the whales. I'm just mixing a drink, or pouring a beer, and trying to make someone's night a little better. That's all I do."

A grin spread across Clay's face and Julia admired the view. He was a fine specimen of man, with a chiseled jawline, and hair that could be held onto hard when you needed to. But more than that, their simple conversation was just that – nice and easy. If someone asked her to define the meaning of life lately, then as far as she could see was to try to be happy as best you could. Right now, she was enjoying the way it was easy to talk to Clay Nichols.

Nothing more. Nothing less.

He wasn't pretentious. He wasn't pushy. He had a directness about himself and what he did for a living that was refreshing.

"To entertainment," she said, raising an empty glass in a toast.

"And to being entertained."

"Let's see if you can keep that up," she said, issuing a challenge, because she craved a distraction like this. The last few months of her life had been far too tightly wound. Too much pressure. Too much trouble. Too many things she shouldn't have to deal with, but was stuck with anyhow. Tonight, she wasn't going to think about all the things chasing her. Tonight was for fun and for admiring the fantastic view. Sometimes, a woman just needed to to flirt off her stress.

"I'm up for it, Julia. I'm definitely up for it."

* * *

That McKenna was right. Hell, she was more than right. Her sister was hot as sin with those curves, those breasts, and the perfect kind of hips that he'd like to get his hands on. Her hair was lush and reddish brown. Her lips were full and ripe for kissing. As well as other things. But more than that, she was feisty, with that smart mouth firing off innuendo with every word. She could dish it out, and she could take it. After the day he'd had, after the way his days went in general, he wanted a night like this.

So they chatted on and off as she served more customers. She asked him about the deal he'd worked on today, and he told her what he could tell. He asked her about the night she'd had, and she nodded to a skinny guy slouched over the corner of the bar, and there was something so easy – so completely lacking in the bullshit and abrasiveness of office hours — about talking to her.

As she mixed up a purple concoction with sugar on the rim, she crooked a finger toward him, signaling for him to lean closer across the bar. He obliged; he wasn't going to complain about being near to her.

"Do you want a Purple Snow Globe, Clay?"

He met her gaze straight on, her green eyes so inviting. "If it's that a drink, no. If Purple Snow Globe is a secret code word for something naughty, I'm game."

"Well played," she said, raising an eyebrow. She eyed the drink she'd just made with a proud sort of look. "It's my signature cocktail. Some day, I'm going to win an award for this bad boy."

He leaned back in the stool and took a slow measured drink from his beer glass, then set it down. "Will I regret not ordering then? For the chance to say I drank a Purple Snow Globe once at a bar in San Francisco?"

She flashed a sexy smile. "It's absolutely delish, so you might regret not tasting it. But I'm glad you didn't order it because it's nothing a man should ever ask for at a bar and expect a woman to want him," she whispered near his ear, her hair brushing his cheek, making him instantly hard. But that wasn't entirely true. He'd been borderline hard for most of the conversation. The feel of her silky strands along the with the words *want him* just ratcheted things up a notch or two.

She stepped away to deliver the drink to a customer and tend to more orders. As she returned to his end of the bar, he picked up where they'd left off. "What do you think a man should drink at a bar?"

"Scotch," she said, punctuating the word with a perfect O shape to her lips. "Or whiskey," she said, her voice a purr now. "Bourbon works too."

"I believe you just named all my favorite drinks."

"I had a feeling you might like those."

"Did you?"

"I always know how to match a drink to a man."

He tapped the side of his beer glass. "Then I'd like to know why I have a beer here in front of me. Tell me that, Julia."

She paused, tilted her head to side with a mischievous flare to her moves, then licked those luscious lips. Damn her; she was hotter than words, and she knew how to play. "When it comes right down to it, a man should drink what the bartender gives him," she said in a sultry voice that made him want to hear her say other things. Lots of other things. Like *Hold me down hard.* Or *Tease me with your tongue.* Yeah, those sorts of things. "That's the best match I can make."

"I don't want you making that match for anyone else then tonight," he said firmly, giving her a hard stare, reminding her that he could play too. Because he knew exactly what he wanted. *Her.* And he didn't want anyone else to have a shot. "Especially because I'm finding the bartender has excellent taste."

She raised an eyebrow. "She does. She has impeccable taste, and she's only making one match tonight," she said, layering her words thick and hot with innuendo.

He wasn't entirely sure where the evening was going next, only because he wasn't the kind of man to take a woman like Julia for granted. He wasn't going to make any sort of assumptions because assumptions got you into trouble in life. He knew that well from his line of work, and from the crap he'd dealt with from his ex, who'd brought heaps of heartache to him in their last few months together before it ended. It was also entirely possibly that Julia was a shameless flirt, angling for a big tip with her saucy little mouth. You couldn't rule anything out, and regardless of where the night ended up, he planned on tipping her well for her bartending work because the woman was doing a hell of a job.

There were other jobs he'd like from her though.

Soon the crowds thinned, and Julia finished up the last call, and then she leaned across the bar, her lips dangerously near his jaw. "You don't have to go when I lock up. In fact, you are more than welcome to stay."

Oh yeah. He was entirely sure where the evening was going now.

CHAPTER THREE

The sound of the lock snapping closed was wholly satisfying. It was the sound of one part of the night ending and another part beginning. A better part. A possibly delectable part.

Call it the no-strings-attached affair that she needed. This man, in town and then heading out of town, seemed like the absolute perfect fit for her.

She could act all prim and demure like she planned to just kiss Clay and send him on his way. But the thought of getting hot and bothered and then forbidding any south of the border activity had zero appeal to her. She was going for him, for all of him. She didn't care if that made her sex-hungry. She *was* hungry for sex. She was jonesing for the kind of roll in the hay that would demolish the tension in her shoulders, let her forget the things she wanted to forget. She had so much trouble in her life, thanks but no thanks to her ex, who'd left town and saddled her with all his problems. Life had been non-stop pressure and worry since then, and she needed a break from it for one night.

Yeah, she was ready to screw the stress right out of her system, and this man seemed the ideal candidate.

Clay was waiting at the bar, tall and hard and sexy as hell in his jeans and button-down shirt. Julia wasn't naive enough to think there was anything deeper going on than a chemical reaction. But what a reaction it was. Her body was drawn to him. His voice affected her, and his dark eyes were so mesmerizing they lured her in. But looks didn't always make for a good lover, did they? No. A good lover took care of a woman, made sure she came first, and then again and again. And Julia could go for an orgasm or two tonight. Maybe even three.

Could this man deliver the goods beyond the surface? Were his hands and his tongue as worthy as the rest of him?

When she returned to him, she didn't mince words. She didn't have time for bullshit, or dating. She was a woman who spoke her mind. "So here's the thing. I've got an idea of how I see the rest of the night playing out. What I'm wondering is if it aligns with yours?"

"Horizontally? That sort of alignment?"

She nodded several times. "I see we're in agreement. So does that mean you're going to put out for me tonight?" she asked with a wicked grin, teasing him with the teenage crudeness of her words.

He cracked up and so did she. Julia liked that he could appreciate her dry and dirty humor.

"Yeah. I think I'll put out for you tonight," he said, then stalked closer, his solid body nearing hers, erasing the space between them as he cupped her cheeks in his hands, and captured her mouth in a hot, wet kiss. It wasn't a slow kiss or a dreamy kiss. No, it was a hungry one that sent a rush of heat flooding her veins. He spun her around, lifted her up on the bar, then edged himself between her legs as he slid his tongue over hers, explored her lips and her mouth as he kissed her hard and furiously. Like she wanted to be kissed, his stubbled jaw rough against her face. He threaded his hands into her hair and he wasn't gentle with his touch, and she thanked her lucky stars for that. Softness was for kittens, pillows and pretty cashmere sweaters. Sex needed to be hard, hot and oh-so-rough around the edges.

She didn't want to be coddled or cuddled. She wanted to take and be taken.

He kissed her greedily and she was sure she'd still be able to feel this kiss tomorrow, in her bones, in her knees. It flared through her whole body like a comet, igniting her. She grabbed his firm ass, yanked him closer until she could feel the full length of his thick cock in her center.

Oh, he had it going on. He definitely more than met her requirements. She rubbed herself against him and he groaned, then broke the kiss, moving his mouth to her ear. "You like that?"

"I do like that."

"You like feeling how hard you made me?"

"I don't like it. I love it," she said.

"I've been rock hard for you all night, Julia. All night, I've been like this."

"That's a long time to be so hard, Clay. I bet you need me to do something about that."

He pulled back to look at her, arching an eyebrow. "Yeah? What do you think I'd like you to do?"

"It's not a matter of what you'd like me to do. It's a matter of what I'm going to do," she said, reaching for his hand that was looped through her hair, freeing it, then bringing his fingers to her face. She drew his index finger into her mouth, wrapping her lips tightly around it, and sucked hard. She watched as his brown eyes filled with heat. Then she pushed her hips against his, grinding against his hard cock, leaving no question as to where she wanted him next. She released his finger and hopped off the counter, missing the press of his body, but wanting to do this her way. She walked behind the bar, reached into her purse, and took out her favorite accessory, dangling her handcuffs for him to see.

She was a woman who knew what she needed, and she needed control.

His brown eyes widened with lust. "You keep handcuffs with you?"

"Never been used. Been waiting for the right man. And I have a feeling you'd like it if I cuffed you right now."

"I'm not going to deny you."

She walked to him and swiveled the stool around, so the wood slats on the back were easier to reach. She grabbed his wrists, pulled them behind him, and cuffed him to the wood. The sound of the metal locking into metal sent a thrill through her. He was hers for now. When so many other things slipped through her fingers like sand – money, hope, her future – *this* she could hold onto. This moment – his pleasure – was in her hands.

"Now, Clay. Tell me. How do you like it?"

"Deep," he growled. "Take me in deep."

"You want to fuck my mouth, you're saying?"

"I would love to fuck that pretty mouth of yours."

She slipped her fingers into the waistband of his jeans, sighing deeply as she felt the hard planes of his belly. She unzipped his jeans, pushed them down to his knees, and marveled at the thick bulge of his cock, the outline of his size deliciously visible though his briefs. Rock hard and all because of how much he wanted her. Heat tore through her as she pressed a hand against his length, palming him.

He hissed as she touched him, his broad chest rising and falling, a dark look of hunger in his eyes. There, that was it. That was what she wanted so badly it sent her body into overdrive – his reaction.

"Now, you're starting something, gorgeous," he said. "And you're going to need to finish it. When you take me in your mouth, you need to take me all the way in."

"Oh, I will. I most definitely will."

She pushed his briefs down, and hot sparks shot straight to her core, turning her molten as she looked at him for the first time. He had a beautiful, majestic cock. Long, thick, and perfectly shaped. She couldn't wait to taste him.

* * *

Clay rolled his head back in pleasure and breathed out hard. This woman was more than fiery. She was scorching and she was a giver, and he couldn't have scripted a better combination as she toyed with him. She gripped him hard in one hand, the way he liked it, squeezing the base, but then teasing the head with her talented tongue, swirling little lines around him that made him want to piston his hips into her lush mouth.

She licked him up and down, lapping him up like a lollipop, all while making the sexiest little murmurs as if she were enjoying it as much as he was. Was that even possible? Because his body was buzzing all over. Then he felt as if electricity had been shocked into his bones when she stopped licking and dived in, taking him all the way in.

"Oh, that's perfect, Julia. Yeah, I want to see those lips of yours nice and tight on me."

She glanced up at him, answered with the wicked look in her pretty green eyes that she intended to ride him hard with her warm mouth.

"You take me in deep, now, okay?"

He might be the one handcuffed, but he still wanted her to know that he liked to be in charge. He couldn't move his hands, and that was a shame because he wanted to pull her head closer to him.

With her lips gripping him, she stroked him with her tongue.

"Keep doing that," he rasped out. "But I want it harder and faster."

She didn't need his direction, but she took it, sucking him in as far as she could. He felt her throat relax as she drew him in, and he loved that she wanted all of him. That she inched her body closer, that she moaned as she tasted him.

"You've got all of me now. But I can't touch your hair with my hands like this, and it's killing me not to grab hard on all that luscious hair," he said as he began thrusting into her. The view of those red lips around his cock sent waves of pleasure through his body, hitting him deep in his bones with the intensity. "So I need you to know that when I take you soon, I'm going to have my hands all wrapped up in your hair and I'll pull harder to make up for what I'm missing right now having my hands cuffed."

She wiggled her eyebrows playfully, then swirled her tongue against his dick. She was the sexiest sight in the world, those gorgeous red lips opened wide and holding on tight. But as much as he wanted to keep watching her, he could barely focus anymore as his climax started to build, and he shuddered. He closed his eyes, rocked into her mouth, and told her what was coming next.

Him.

"I'm going to come any second. And I'm going to come in your mouth. That all right with you?"

She nodded and sucked harder, stroking him with her hand, all while keeping him far inside her delicious mouth. Then she grabbed his ass hard with her other hand, pulling him even closer as his orgasm tore through him, and she swallowed his release.

When he recovered the power of speech, he told her he needed a Purple Snow Globe.

Stat.

* * *

Julia had never been pinned with her own bra before. But here she was, spread out on one of the leather lounge chairs in the back of the bar, her hands above her head, the silky straps digging into her flesh. That man knew how to tie some serious knots. After buttoning his jeans, Clay had proceeded to take the reins. He undressed her quickly, stripping her down to nothing, his eyes raking her over as he tugged off her sweater, her jeans, her bra and then her panties, inhaling sharply when she stood naked in front of him, savoring the view before he laid her on the chair and quickly tied her own pink lace bra around her wrists.

"I liked that bra, you know," she said.

"It'll still work."

"Are you sure?"

"Do I look like the kind of man who would rip such a pretty pink bra?"

She shook her head. "I bet you are the kind of man who could take it off with his teeth."

"I might do just that next time."

"No cuffs for me?"

"Think of me like MacGyver. I use other tools," he said with a glint in his eyes.

"Fine. I'm all for equal opportunity bondage."

"And I'm all for equal opportunity oral." He kissed her mouth hard, silencing any more of her quips. But he quickly broke the contact. "Now where's that Purple Snow Globe you just made?"

She tipped her chin to the table next to them, eager to see what he had in mind for the drink he swore he'd never touch.

He reached for the glass, holding up the purple drink with raspberry juice, gin and her secret ingredient, then sugared on the rim. His lips quirked up in a grin. "Now I won't have any regrets about not ordering this, though I believe this is the only way I'd want to drink a Purple Snow Globe," he said, then carefully tipped the edge of the glass above Julia's breasts, letting some of the liquid spill between them. She shivered as the droplets slid down her belly. Clay bent his head between her breasts and licked up the dark liquid.

"Mmmm. That is an award-winning drink," he growled against her skin, and she writhed into him. He raised his head and poured more of the drink on her belly. Some of it spilled onto the lounge chair, but he quickly captured the rest with his tongue. A ripple of desire tore through her as he touched her. She wished her hands were free so she could push his head between her legs where she wanted him. Where she was dying for him. She desperately wanted to grab hard onto his hair, pull him into her, and let him plunder her with his tongue. She ached for his touch, and she was turned on beyond any and all reason.

But he had other plans, inching up to her breasts, cupping them in his big strong hands.

"Your breasts are gorgeous, and I bet you'd like it if I bite down just a little bit," he whispered roughly against her skin, and his sexy words made her even more fevered. He flicked his tongue against her nipple, drawing it deeper into his mouth until she cried out. Then he bit down. Not so hard it hurt, but hard enough that it hurt so good.

"That feels incredible," she moaned.

"Good." He licked a wet path between her breasts, squeezing them as he brought the other one into his mouth, sucking hard on her nipple til it was a diamond point in his mouth. Her hips shot up, her body nearly begging for relief. Every flicker, every touch of his tongue on her drove her wild, sending sparks through all her cells. He drew her nipple across his teeth, slowly, so torturously slowly that she cried out. "*Please.*"

"I can do so much more to you with my mouth."

"I want it," she panted. "I want to know all the things you can do with your mouth."

"Then I'll have to stop talking and start eating," he said, looking up at her holding her lustful gaze with his own dark, hooded one.

"You better," she said, and gasped as he settled between her legs, his strong shoulders against her thighs. He licked her once, swirling his tongue against her wetness. She arched her hips instantly, her body terribly desperate for his touch, for contact where she wanted him most. He pulled back to look at her.

"More, please," she said playfully.

"You like that?"

"Uh, yeah."

"I need you to spread your legs then, Julia. I can't go down on you the way I want until your legs are wide open."

Heat surged in her body as he dirty talked her.

"How far?"

She let her knees fall open, watching his reaction. His eyes grew darker, as he stared greedily at her center. She'd never wanted a man to go down on her more than she did in this instant. She was dying for his mouth. She wanted to feel his lips and let him work his magic tongue on her. She wanted to let go, to give in to the moment, to the night, to the tantalizing possibility of coming hard and good with him.

She needed it; the blinding wave of getting lost in release, the druggy bliss of pleasure and how it could drown out all your troubles, at least temporarily, and leave you awash in intoxication for a spell.

"I want you wide open for me. I want to see how far you can spread your legs," he said, pressing his hands on the inside of her thighs and pushing her legs apart.

She felt helpless with her wrists pinned over her head, as he opened her legs into a wide V. She was submitting to him, trusting him with her pleasure – naked, tied and spread on the leather chaise lounge.

"I need to make sure you keep your thighs wide open for me because that's how I like it. You think you can come from just my tongue? Because I'm not going to use my fingers," he said roughly, in a challenging tone, then flicked his tongue against her wetness to demonstrate what he could do with his tongue alone. The feeling of him was so astonishing she groaned loudly, wriggling her hips. "Yeah, I think I can come from your tongue."

"You sure? Because I want to save the inside of you for my cock. It's going to be hard for me to hold back, but I can do it. Can you?" he asked again as he pressed a hot wet kiss between her legs.

She moaned and rocked into him. "Yes. Your tongue is amazing."

"You have to do it my way, Julia." With a firm grip on her legs, he licked up the side of her thigh, causing her to shudder, then move her legs reflexively.

"Keep them open, gorgeous," he commanded. "If you close your legs, I'll stop."

"I'll keep my legs spread," she said in a raspy voice she barely recognized as her own. Hell, she barely recognized herself, she was so overcome with lust and the aching need for him. "I will."

"You listen to me, and I'll make you writhe and moan. If you don't listen, I will have to stop and wait until you can follow orders," he said sharply, staring hard at her, his brown eyes making it clear he was in charge. "Don't make me wait. I don't want to wait. I want to taste you so badly it's killing me."

"I'll listen because I can't wait either," she said, surprised how she'd shifted from the badass woman on her knees with his thick cock in her mouth, to the submissive, giving over her pleasure to this man she barely knew. But sometimes that was the point of being with someone you barely knew. Because you could give in to the purity of the physical. She was in that zone now; she wanted to stay there all night long. If that made her submissive, or bad, or sex-crazed, fine. She'd take any and all of those adjectives heaped on her. But right now, all she knew was *want*, and that was all she wanted to know.

To hell with her problems, her troubles, her past. To hell with her ex and to all she owed. To hell with everything else but *this*.

He pressed his tongue against her wetness, licking her, swirling delicious lines across her core. She angled her hips closer to his mouth, gasping in delirious pleasure as he kissed her hard and licked her. He explored her, sensually, deliberately, consuming her as if she were the best thing he'd ever tasted. That's how he made her feel with the sounds that rumbled low in his throat as he stroked his tongue across her.

He lavished attention on her clit and she screamed in pleasure, futilely trying to grasp at something, anything, with her tied-up hands – just to hold on – as he buried his tongue inside her.

She arched her hips as the sensations shot through her, hard and fast, like quicksilver tearing through her blood and veins. The feelings were so intense from his delicious mouth making love to her, and his hands holding her down hard, making her open and completely vulnerable. She had no choice but to let him go down on her however he wanted. He was masterful with his lips and his tongue, licking her clit while kissing her pussy senseless. Her pulse raced, her blood roared. Soon, she started to lose control, rocking into him recklessly. She wanted to pull him close, but her hands were pinned, and she liked it that way. No, she *reveled* in it – as the waves of ecstasy slammed into her, crashing into every corner, flooding her inside and out.

She shuddered and moaned, saying his name over and over. As the feelings ebbed, he tugged her close and kissed her cheek. Her forehead. Her neck. Even her nose.

Soft, sweet, fluttery kisses.

Her body felt like a noodle. She was warm and glowing, in that heady state after an epic orgasm. He seemed to sense that she needed a minute to bask in the aftereffects. Gently, he untied her hands as he buzzed his soft lips from her throat to her ear.

"Did you like it when my face was between your legs, Julia?"

His voice was low and soft, and there was a tender tone to it. So different from the rough way he'd talked to her when he issued his instructions. She pressed closer to him, savoring the momentary sweetness, loving that he had so many sides – hard and hungry, then gentle when he needed to be. He ran a hand down her side, across her waist, traveling to her hip. He bent his head to her belly, layering a soft kiss there, then over to her hipbone. She could get used to this kind of touch, to how he knew when to hit each note.

"I loved it," she murmured.

"Good. Because you taste fantastic on me," he said, then claimed her mouth in a quick, hot kiss. "And now you taste fantastic on you."

She looped her hands into his thick hair and wrapped her legs around his hips, letting him know what she wanted next. "Can you please sleep with me now?"

He raised an eyebrow. "You ready to feel me inside you?"

"God yes," she said. "But you need to get naked like I am." She quickly unbuttoned his shirt and pushed down his jeans.

He pulled her up from the chair, looked deep into her eyes, then raked her over from head to toe. "I am so glad I walked into your bar this evening, because this is the best night I've had in a long time, and you are quite possibly a perfect woman. So as far as I can see, the only thing that could possibly make it better is you bent over the chair with your ass in the air."

She hitched in a breath as a ribbon of desire was unleashed in her body. "I want it hard, Clay," she told him as she turned around and bent over, lifting her bottom for him. "I want it hard and deep and I want to feel your cock all the way inside me."

He fished in his wallet for a condom, rolled it on, and smacked her ass once.

"You will feel me for days, gorgeous."

* * *

That back.

So long and sexy and smooth. That hair. All silky and thick and perfect for tugging. But that ass. It was so inviting. Clay rubbed his palms against her smooth, soft skin, then placed a thumb on each cheek to spread her open. Her pussy was glistening and his cock twitched eagerly at the sight; the jumpy fucker was ready to be inside her, but he wanted to enjoy the view as he entered. She'd tasted delicious, so hot and sexy and willing, but maybe she tasted so good to him because she liked it the same way he did. She liked to dominate and to be dominated. She liked to talk dirty, and be talked dirty to. She was a scorching combination of everything he'd ever craved in the bedroom – never had he met a woman before that he'd clicked with in every way – and now he was was going to have her how he wanted. He teased her wet lips with the head of his cock. She whimpered, then raised her ass higher.

"You like how my cock feels against you? You want me inside you?"

"Yes, I don't want you to tease me. I want you to take me," she said in a firm tone, turning her head to shoot him a sharp stare.

"You telling me what to do, gorgeous?"

"Yes. I'm telling you what to do. And you better take me now because I don't want to be teased."

He rubbed himself against her, and her body responded instantly, shivering as he toyed with her. "But it seems you like teasing," he said playfully as she pushed back against him.

"Clay, please," she said, as if she desperately needed him to put her out of her pent-up misery.

"You gonna beg for it?"

"No," she said, reverting to her tough stance. "I don't want to beg for it. If you make me beg, I will go take care of myself."

He smacked her ass for that impudence. But he loved her feisty attitude; it shot sparks through his whole body. "I would love to watch you touch yourself," he said as he pushed the tip of his cock inside her.

"You think I'd let you watch?"

"Oh, gorgeous. You'd love it if I watched. You'd get even wetter with my eyes on you as you fingered yourself. Are you good at making yourself come, Julia?" he asked, sliding in another inch and rolling his eyes back in his head at the feel of her hot flesh surrounding him.

"So good at it. I will make myself come in seconds if you don't fuck me deep right now," she said, looking back at him, her green eyes fiery and demanding as she taunted. "Maybe I'll even torture you by letting you watch."

"I fully intend to take you up on that kind of torture sometime," he said. But not now. Because right now he wanted to be buried deep inside her more than he wanted to tease her, toy with her, control her. "But right now, you're getting what you want."

Screw teasing. Screw taking it slow. He sank into her and they groaned in unison. She felt extraordinary, so tight against him.

She braced herself with her hands on the back of the lounge chair. "You feel amazing," she murmured, and that made him even harder, hearing her unfettered reaction. No saucy talking back, no snappy mouth. Not that he didn't love those things. He did. A hell of a lot. But to hear those simple words escape her throat turned him on fire.

"*Clay*," she groaned as he rocked into her, stroking in and out, hitting her far and deep, then pulling almost all the way out. Only to pound into her again.

"Is this what you wanted when you looked at me with those fuck-me eyes behind the bar?" he whispered roughly, holding her hips hard as he slammed back into her.

"Yes," she cried out.

"Did you picture bending over for me and letting me take you? Letting me own you with my cock so far inside you?"

He thrust into her again, and she wriggled her ass. Such a beautiful sight, that smooth creamy skin. He rubbed his palms against the soft perfect globes. He wanted to bite it, to sink his teeth into the sweet flesh and leave a mark on her, but there would be time for that later. For now, this woman needed a good hard fucking that would radiate through her beautiful body for days.

"I was just hoping you'd be eight inches," she said, and he could practically hear the smirk in her voice.

He thrust hard into her, making her cry out. Then he stopped his movements, remaining still and deep in her. He bent over her, his strong chest against her sexy back, and he gripped a fistful of her hair. Then he licked the shell of her ear. "More than eight inches, gorgeous. Don't ever doubt that."

She drew in a sharp breath. "Pull my hair," she said, and he did, tugging hard.

Then he drove into her again, each thrust reminding her of what more than eight inches felt like. Her cries grew louder and her breathing more erratic. He reached his other hand around to touch her clit. Fast, quick strokes while he buried himself deeper in her. His own climax started to build.

"I'm going to come soon, Julia. But you need to come first. I want you to come so badly. I've wanted it just as much as you wanted me inside you. Tell me how much you wanted me," he said, sliding his thumb across her as she trembled and bucked her hips against him.

"Yes, I wanted you so badly. And I wanted you to make me come, and now you are. You are making me come," she said in a broken, breathy voice. He let go of her hair, cupped her chin and turned her face to him so he could watch as he brought her to the other side, her eyes squeezing shut, her mouth forming a perfect O, that first silent moan. Then, she screamed out loudly, his name echoing around the bar, and he chased her orgasm with his own, groaning as the pleasure ripped through him, tearing through ever damn cell in his body, lighting him up with electricity. Then they collapsed onto the lounge, a sweaty tangled mess of limbs and flesh. He pulled her close, spooning her, and kissed her earlobe.

"Come back to my hotel. Spend the night with me," he said softly. "I want to curl up with you. I want to wake up with you. I want to make love to you before I leave."

She shivered and breathed out hard.

"Yes."

CHAPTER FOUR

Later that night, Julia lay in Clay's arms, blissed out and sleepily content from her third orgasm of the evening. The man had delivered on every promise. When he'd told her he planned to make love to her, he wasn't kidding. Back at the hotel, he'd worshipped her body, layering kisses all over her from head to toe – yes, he even sucked on a toe, and it felt exquisite – and then he'd entered her. It had been one of those lingering, unhurried and wickedly wonderful sessions. Her legs wrapped around his back, him taking his time with long, tantalizing thrusts, rolling his hips in and out, all the while kissing her neck, her face, her breasts. The man could fuck and the man could make love. He could give her orders, and he could take her direction. He could yank hard on her hair, and blaze a trail of sweet kisses against her damp skin.

Now, he snuggled with her, tucking her against his big, strong body. His toned arm was draped under her breasts, giving her a fantastic view of his tattoo, a tribal arm band around his left bicep with strong, curved strokes. She ran her fingers along the design, tracing it. "I like this. When did you have it done?"

"Thank you. Did it after law school to remind myself why I do what I do."

"How does this remind you?"

"It symbolizes passion. The thing I always want to bring to my job, to my life, to everything."

"I'd say you have passion in spades," she said, pressing her body closer to his so she could feel his smooth, flat belly against her back. The perfect position for apres-sex. "Mmm....this is nice," he said, brushing a soft, quick kiss on her shoulder. "I'm glad I met you."

"Me too," she murmured.

"Tell me something about you I don't know."

"Well, that would be almost everything, wouldn't it?"

He laughed. "I know plenty about you already. I just want to know more."

"Tell me what you know already."

"I know you're tough as nails, that you don't take shit from anyone, that you can size people up in a second."

"That's my job. Any good bartender worth her salt can do that."

"And you're excellent at it. I also know you take pride in your work. Even though you're not saving the world you like being good at what you do."

She shrugged against him. "I suppose that's true."

"So there. I know stuff about you already." He snuggled her closer, drawing lazy lines across her belly as they talked. "I also know you're daring, and not afraid to speak your mind, and that you have a healthy sexual appetite."

She smiled, and elbowed him playfully. "I do, but don't think I get around because I don't. You're the first man I've been with in a year."

"You've been with women in between then?" he asked, in a teasing tone.

"Ha ha. But not what I meant. Though I'm sure you wouldn't mind."

"I absolutely would not mind watching you eat pussy one bit. In fact, I'm going to add that to my bucket list. You, and all that gorgeous red hair spread out across a pair of sexy thighs as you lick and kiss and suck..."

She shook her head and laughed. "You are trouble. All I was saying is that I don't do this often. I don't hookup with men who come to my bar."

"I came in your bar too," he added, making Julia snicker once again. The moonlight shone through the window that overlooked the streets of San Francisco, and the white gauzy curtain blew gently in the night breeze. Outside the door, she was vaguely aware of a cart being rolled, which meant room service some-where on the floor was being delivered. Maybe to an-other pair of new lovers who were famished after the best kind of workout. But even if there were other lovers nearby, she knew – beyond a shadow of a doubt – that no one else had this kind of mind-blow-ing chemistry. She and Clay were electric. "Anyway, I don't do this either. It's not a habit. You have to know you're irresistible, Julia. *Irresistible*," he repeated.

With that one word, her heart beat the tiniest bit faster; maybe it even started to leap. And a part of her wanted to bolt for having the single tiniest little feel-ing beyond the physical. But another part of her wanted to bask in that feeling a little more.

"So are you," she whispered.

He ran his strong fingers through her hair, touching her softly. "Now, let's go back to the start of this con-versation. I want you tell me something about you. You're not getting out of this so easily."

She wriggled her rear against him. "I wasn't trying to. What do you want to know?"

"What do you like to read?"

She smiled in the dark. She liked that he'd asked first about books, rather than movies or TV, the world he trafficked in. "Books," she said dryly.

"What kind of books, Little Miss Sarcastic?"

"Adventure stories," she said, and she could practi-cally feel him raise an eyebrow inquisitively. She shifted to her other side so she could face him as they talked. He shot her a quizzical look, as if the breaking of the physical contact perturbed him. He solved the problem quickly, reaching out to touch her, running his hand down her thigh.

"Can't keep your hands off me?"

"No, I can't. And I see no reason not to touch you. What kind of adventure stories?"

"Real adventures. Scary adventures. Like the ship captain who was held hostage by Somali pirates."

"A Captain's Duty," he said, and she was impressed he knew the title of the book, rather than simply the title for the film based on it. "Good book. Good movie too, Captain Phillips. What else?"

"Stories about SEALS."

"The fictional ones where they're back from their missions and they fall in love with the hot woman they're assigned to protect?"

"No," she said, laughing.

"Wait. The ones where they fall for the physical therapist who rehabs them after war?"

Another laugh. "My my, don't you know everything about romance tropes? But no, I mean the real ones about their real missions."

"That's it. You're going to have to stop talking now. Because if you say anything more it's going to become clear you are the most perfect woman ever made."

"And why is that? You a fan of SEAL stories too?"

"I'm a fan of you growing more fascinating with every detail I learn."

"I'm an onion. Keep peeling me."

"A sexy onion. Let me take off another layer," he said and bent his head to her shoulder, nibbling playfully.

"What about you?"

"What about me? What do I like to read?"

"No. I'm picking a different topic. What movies do you like? And don't name your clients' films."

"Of course, their works are all my favorites. But when I'm not watching their movies, I like heist flicks."

"Like Ocean's Eleven?"

He nodded. "Best heist movie ever."

"And The Italian Job?"

"Another excellent one."

"And Thomas Crowne Affair?"

"Brilliant plot."

"And Die Hard?"

"Seen it ten times. Maybe more," Clay said.

"I love them all too," she said.

"Okay, now you have to cease speaking."

"Because that makes me perfect?" she joked.

"Something like that," he muttered as he pulled her in close, and kissed her once more.

* * *

When she woke up the next morning, Clay ran a hand through his hair, then cleared his throat. "I can push back my flight until later tonight. Do you want to spend the day with me?"

She couldn't think of a better idea. "And we can talk more about movies, and TV shows, and books?"

"That. Or about the threesome we're going to have some day."

She arched an eyebrow. "I am not sharing you."

He smiled devilishly at her. "Good answer. And for the record, I would never ever share you."

"Good. Now for even suggesting that, I need two orgasms, stat."

He tipped his forehead to the bathroom. "Shower. You. Against the wall."

After he delivered on her request, they went out to lunch in Hayes Valley at one of her favorite restaurants that had 47 varieties of dipping sauce for French Fries. Clay agreed that it might be the best restaurant he'd ever been to and that fries were an unbeatable food choice.

But as the evening unspooled, Julia became aware of a ticking clock. Time seemed to speed up, to charge headfirst to the end of the night as the inevitable goodbye loomed closer. When his car arrived to take him to the airport, she said goodbye and planted a quick kiss on his cheek. There would be no poignant, postcard kind of kiss. They might have had fun, they might be insanely compatible in bed, they might even have the same taste in movies and books, but there was no *they*. She had too much baggage here in her hometown. Too much trouble that wasn't close to being wrapped up. And too many more Tuesday nights before she could call it even.

She needed to start erecting a wall. Clay would go down in her history as the best sex ever – a night of unbridled perfection in the bedroom. And, fine, he scored major points for being easy to talk to and fun to spend the day with. But he lived 3000 miles away.

"Nice meeting you," she said crisply and turned to leave.

He grabbed her wrist and pulled her to him, her body flush with his. Damn, she loved the feel of his strong chest against hers. She liked it too much.

"Julia," he said, and this time his voice was intense, serious. "I had an amazing time with you. I know this sounds crazy since we live on opposite coasts, but I need to see you again. I'm going to call you."

He kissed her deeply, a searing kiss that made her stand on her tip toes and thread her hands in his hair so she could hold on tight. When he broke the kiss, she felt wobbly and her lips missed his.

As he drove off, she realized maybe her heart missed him too. But she reminded herself that it was easy to say *I'm going to call you.* What was harder was doing that. What was Herculean was seeing someone on the other side of the country.

* * *

Clay pounded hard on the punching bag with a final hit. His breath came fast, his heart beating ferociously from the workout.

"Never seen you hit so hard, man," Davis said to him. "Who are you picturing now? That network bastard you had to deal with in San Francisco?"

Clay shook his head as he bent over the water fountain at the boxing gym for a cold drink of water. He hadn't been picturing the network exec at all. He'd been thinking of how much it sucked that Julia lived so damn far away. He'd been back in New York for one day. One stinking day, and he couldn't get that feisty woman out of his mind.

"No," he answered crisply.

"You should just call her," Davis said.

He snapped his head up, staring hard at his friend. "What?"

"The woman you spent the extra day with in San Francisco."

"How did you know?"

"You told me you were coming back in the morning and you missed our workout yesterday." He tapped the side of his head. "Remember? I know how to read people. It's my job."

"Anyway," Clay said, trying to brush him off.

"Are you going to?"

"Call her?"

"Yeah. Call her. Because you should."

Shrugging, he tried to act cool and casual. But the truth was he'd always been planning to call her. He hadn't been giving her a line when he left the other night. He wanted to see her again and discover if there was something more to them. He'd enjoyed talking to her as much as he'd enjoyed making her scream his name. She fascinated him, and he couldn't let her be just one night. He wanted more nights with her.

When he reached his apartment and shut the door behind him, he dialed her number. She answered on the second ring.

"Hello, person I never thought I'd hear from again."

He smiled, wishing he could tug her sweet little body against his, plant a kiss on her beautiful face, feel her melt into his touch.

"Hey, Julia. What would you say about coming to New York for the weekend? I have a new set of ropes I've been meaning to use, and a restaurant I want to try, and a big king-size bed you'd look spectacular tied up to. Oh, and there's also a new heist movie coming out this weekend that we could see."

She laughed once. "Let me get this straight. I'm being invited to the Big Apple for dinner, a movie and a little bondage?"

"Yes, that would be correct."

* * *

She didn't answer right away. She carefully considered his request.

She'd won big earlier that night. The kind of win that made the weight of her past start to lessen. Besides, he was only asking for two nights of her life. This wasn't a commitment. This wasn't a relationship, and she sure as hell wasn't going to get caught up in him.

"Then the answer is pick me up at the airport in a town car, handsome, because I'm going to be ready for all of that and then some as soon as I step off the plane," she said, as she sank down on her couch, kicked off her heels, and started counting down the hours til the weekend.

It was one weekend. Nothing more, she promised herself.

They stayed on the phone for an hour, talking about everything and nothing, and his voice lowered to that sexy growl as he asked her what she was wearing. Then, he brought her there again.

Just a weekend, she repeated the next day, and the next, and the next, and all during the flight, and even as she walked through the terminal and out the doors of LaGuardia.

But when she saw him in that hot-as-sin suit, with his tie already loosened, and sunglasses on, leaning against the town car, she had a feeling she'd never want the weekend to end....

NIGHT AFTER NIGHT

"Clay Nichols is the perfect man. He treats his woman like a queen and would do anything for her, but he's totally up for f*&ing her like a porn star." —Jen at Sub Club

This book is dedicated to my good friends
Cara, Hetty and Kim. You are my naughty-planning
committee, and this book would quite simply
not exist without the three of you.

CHAPTER ONE

The ace of diamonds was solo.

Such a shame, because it would look fantastic paired with, say, an ace of clubs, spades or hearts. But this was the hand she'd been dealt and it was ace high, nothing more. They were down to three still standing for this round: Julia, the Trust Fund Baby, and then New Guy. His name was Hunter; he was a beanpole and his hair was short, spiky and blond. He wore khaki pants and a plaid shirt, and had twitchy fingers. Probably because there was a no-cell-phone rule during the game, and he was missing out on emails from his *team,* Julia guessed.

She bet he was an Internet startup type, maybe a venture capitalist. He was used to risks; he liked to take them. That's why he'd been brought to this game, recruited specifically to play with her. But the trouble was—well, trouble for him—he laughed when he bluffed. Julia spotted it early, and then tracked it.

He'd done it with a pair of fives a couple of rounds back that she'd easily beat with two jacks. He'd chuckled softly too with his king high a few hands ago.

Bless that newbie. He couldn't even hide his tell, and Julia could kiss him if he kept this up because it made her job so much easier.

"Five hundred," he said confidently, pushing another black chip into the pile as he cleared his throat. Julia was a panther poised for prey; muscles taut and frozen, lying in wait for the sign.

Then it came. It started in his nose, like a small, playful snort, then traveled to his belly, and finally turned into a quick, rumbly laugh.

Ah, brilliant. She could smell potential victory in the air. Of course, she could also smell the pork dumplings and pepper steak from Mr. Pong's downstairs. When she'd first started coming here, to this second-floor apartment parked atop a restaurant in China Town that smelled of takeout even when pizza had been ordered for the games, she was sure she'd never remove the stench from her clothes, much less her nostrils. Perma-scent. But she'd had no problems in the laundry department and as for her nose, well, now she was used to the smell that permeated every pore on Tuesday nights.

She never ate here, especially not with the bulldozer-sized heavy who stood guard over the game in the kitchen. She knew his name, but who cared what it was? To her he was simply Skunk; he had one streak of white in his dyed-black hair. His meaty fingers were jammed into the coldcut plate, pawing through the leftover slices of deli meat. Julia wanted to roll her eyes, crinkle her nose, or shoot him a hard stare.

She knew better, though, for many reasons, not the least of which was the square outline of the handle of the Glock poking at the hem of his pants. He'd never pulled it, but the gun was an omnipresent reminder that a bullet could be unleashed at a moment's notice. She shivered inside at the thought, but outside she showed no emotion, not toward Skunk, not toward Hunter the pawn, and certainly none for Trust Fund Baby when he shrugged, blew a long stream of air through his lips, and slammed his cards down. He held his hands out wide. "I'm out."

Then there were two.

She eyed the pot, her hand, and the newbie.

Her heart thumped, and a fleet of nerves ghosted through her, but only briefly.

Don't let on.

She had no tells. Her face was stone. She'd mastered the impassive look a long time ago. She could fake her way through anything. *A perfect liar*, the ninth-grade school guidance counselor had declared when Julia denied punching Amelia Cartwright in the nose after Amelia had called another girl a nasty name.

"Did you just hit Amelia Cartwright?"

"No," Julia had said. She didn't shuffle her feet. She didn't look away. She'd lied like it was the truth and that had served her well ever since then.

Perfect lie = perfect truth.

She plucked out a black chip from her stack, then another, rolling them back and forth between the pads of her thumb and index finger, her fire-engine red nails long and lacquered. The nails were part of the look—low-cut tops, tight jeans and four-inch black pumps for every game. The regulars knew her, but the new players never took a woman seriously, especially when she dressed like it was girls' night out.

That's why newbies were brought in. So she could hustle them. It was better that they underestimated her.

"I'll raise you $500," she said in an emotionless voice, sliding two chips into the pile.

This was the moment. Nerves like steel. Blood like ice.

Hunter sucked in a deep breath, like he was trying to inhale thick malt from a thin straw. He stared longingly at the pile of chips in the middle of the table, chewed on the corner of his lip, and glanced at his cards one last time.

"I'm out," he said, slapping the cards down on the scratched-up table that reeked of noodles, beer and regret. If tables could talk, this one could tell stories of all the wedding bands lost and sports cars gained here, all the highs and lows it witnessed.

"Then I'll take this," she said, not needing to reveal her ace high as she reached across the table and gathered up the pot.

She stood, walked straight to Skunk, and handed him the chips. "I'll cash out."

He stuffed a rolled-up slice of bologna between his thick lips, inhaled the meat, then licked off his stubby fingers before he counted out her money. Nearly five thousand, and she wanted to sing, to shout, to soar.

"You want me to give this to Charlie?"

She shook her head. "I will."

"I'll walk you downstairs."

As if she were going anyplace else but to deliver the dough.

Still, Skunk followed her, serving as her handcuffs, huffing as he waddled down the steps.

"You played good tonight," he said in between heavy breaths.

"Thanks," she said, wishing she'd liked playing so well. Like she once did. She used to love poker like there was no tomorrow, a true favorite past time. Now it was tainted.

"I'm proud of you," he said, patting her on the back.

Inside, she recoiled at his touch. On the outside, she acted like it was no big deal. Like none of this was a big deal.

A minute later, they weaved through the tables to the back of Mr. Pong's restaurant, mostly empty at this late hour. Tall and trim, Charlie was hunched over in a chair, swiping his finger across the screen of his iPad. He wore a sharp black suit, a white shirt and no tie. He smiled when he saw her, baring his teeth, yellowed from smoking.

The sight of him made her skin crawl.

His eyes traveled up and down her body hungrily. She pretended he wasn't undressing her in his mind as she turned over the cash. "Here."

"Ah, it's my favorite color. Green from Red," he said, stroking the cash.

She told him the number. "Count it."

"I trust you, Red." His accent was some sort of mix of Greek and Russian. Not Chinese, though, despite the headquarters in China Town. From the little bits and pieces she had cobbled together he both liked Chinese food, and had taken over this restaurant and the apartment above it. Probably from some poor schmuck who'd owed him, too. Someone who didn't make good on a debt.

"I don't trust you though," she said sharply.

"Funny," he said as he laughed, then counted the bills because there was no trust between either of them. "Very funny. Do you tell jokes that funny when you are working behind your bar? Or should I drop by sometime to check?"

Red clouds passed before her eyes. Julia clenched her fists, channeling her anger into her hands as she bit her tongue. She knew better than to incite him.

Still, she hated it when Charlie mentioned her bar, hated it almost as much as his unplanned visits to Cubic Z. Drop-ins, he called them. Like a restaurant inspector, popping in whenever he wanted.

"You are welcome anytime at my bar," she said through gritted teeth.

"I know," he said pointedly. "And the next time I'm there, the pretty bartender will make me a pretty drink."

When he was done counting, he dropped his hand into the pocket of his pants, slowly rooted around, and withdrew a slender knife. Only a few inches long and more like a camping tool, it was hardly a weapon, but it didn't need to possess firepower to send the message—he could cut her to pieces if she failed to deliver. He brought the handle of the knife to his chin, scratched his jaw once, twice, like a dog with fleas, keeping his muddy-brown eyes on her the whole time in a sharp, taut line. He didn't blink. He shoved the knife back into his pocket, then raised his hand and snapped his fingers. Some kind of business goon scurried over, a leather-bound ledger tucked under his arm. "I knew you could take the VC," Charlie said to her, a nefarious glint in his eye. "That's why we brought Hunter for you. You did a good job, separating the fool from his money." Julia's insides twisted with the way Charlie talked. Then he turned to his associate who'd opened the book. "Mark this down in the books. Red is a little bit closer."

The guy scribbled in a number.

"A lot closer," Julia corrected.

"A lot. A little. What's the difference? The only thing that matters—" Charlie stopped to raise a finger in the air, then come swooping down with it, like a pelican eyeing prey as he stabbed her name in the ledger "—is when this says zero. Until then, you are a lot, you are a little, you are mine. Now, you want some kung pao chicken? It's considered the best in San Francisco by all the critics."

She shook her head. "No thanks. I've had my fill tonight."

"I will see you next Tuesday, then. Shall I send one of my limos for you?"

"I'll walk."

She turned on her heels and left, walking home in the cool San Francisco night, leaving Charlie and his chicken behind her.

When she returned to her apartment, she tried to push the game out of her mind as she let the door slam. She washed her hands, poured herself a glass of whiskey, and was about to reach for the remote so she could lose herself in some mindless TV when her phone rang. A 917 number flashed across the screen. Her heart dared to flutter. Dumb organ. Then her belly flipped. Stupid stomach.

But it was two against three because only her common sense said *Don't answer*, and common sense wasn't winning. The brain rarely bested the body. The caller was Clay Nichols who she'd met a few days ago while she was tending bar. The tall, dark, gorgeous, filthy-mouthed lawyer from New York, who fucked like a champion and called her irresistible, and then asked her to tell him more about all the things she liked as they lay tangled up in hotel sheets, blissed out.

The man who lived three thousand miles away. The man she was sure was full of shit when he'd said he would call her again. The man she'd spent some of the best twenty-four hours of her life with.

She answered on the second ring. "Hello, person I never thought I'd hear from again."

"Hey, Julia. What would you say about coming to New York for the weekend?"

A smile started to form on her lips. "Tell me why I would want to go to New York for the weekend," she said, sinking down on her couch, crossing her ankles.

"For starters, I have a new set of ropes I've been meaning to use, and a restaurant I want to try, and a big king-size bed you'd look spectacular tied up to. Oh, and there's also a new heist movie coming out this weekend that we could see."

She laughed. "Let me get this straight. I'm being invited to the Big Apple for dinner, a movie, and a little bondage?"

"Yes, that would be correct."

She didn't answer right away. Her mind flashed back to her big win tonight. Regardless of the chains

Charlie had on her, she *was* closer. And while she'd promised herself she wouldn't get involved with anyone till she was free, Clay wasn't asking for more than two nights of her life. Two nights were thoroughly finite, and therefore could be thoroughly enjoyed. She had off this weekend. Besides, the very thought of Clay had a way of erasing some of the evening, of blotting out those moments when she was so clearly under Charlie's thumb.

"Then the answer is, pick me up at the airport in a town car, handsome, because I'm going to be ready for all of that and then some as soon as I step off the plane," she said, as she kicked off her heels, and took a drink of her whiskey, enjoying the burn as the liquor slid down her throat.

They chatted for longer, and soon the tone shifted, and his voice lowered. "What are you wearing right now?"

"What do you want me to be wearing?"

"Thigh-high white stockings, lacy white panties, and a matching bra," he answered immediately.

"And what would you do if I were wearing that?"

"Drive you crazy through the lace with my tongue, then take your panties off with my teeth."

She didn't think it was the whiskey that was making her feel warm all over. "Funny thing, Clay. I believe that's what I'll be wearing on Friday afternoon."

The next day, she went lingerie shopping.

* * *

Carefully, so as not to run the nylon, Julia inched the stocking up her thigh. Her sister sat perched on a peach-colored armchair in the corner of the spacious dressing room of Hetty's Secret Closet on Union Street. McKenna absently kicked her ankle back and forth, a pleasantly distracting sight because her heels were sparkly peacock blue, matching her sapphire-colored skirt.

"What do you think?" Julia asked as she twirled around to give a full view of the bra, panty and stocking set.

A well-known fashion blogger and online video star, her sister has suggested this chic boutique for the shopping trip. Now, McKenna surveyed her up and down, pressing a finger to her lips as if she were studiously considering the undergarments in question. "It's a good thing you don't get cold easily. It's chilly in New York in April. I was just there."

Julia rolled her eyes. "It's not as if I'm going to strut around the Big Apple in this get-up only," she said, gesturing to her lingerie ensemble.

"I'm just checking," she said with a wink. "You'll pair it with what? A trench coat?"

"No. This thing called a skirt. Ever heard of it? Then a blouse, too. Then the trench coat."

"I am pleased to inform you," her sister began, flashing a bright smile, "you have the Fashion Hound seal of approval on your sexy outfit."

"Exactly why I keep you around." Julia began stripping off the stockings, the underwear and the bra.

"Wait. Don't I get a little sashay of the hips and all? A lap dance maybe?"

"I'm saving that all for Friday, Saturday and Sunday."

"You must really like this guy if he gets your whole weekend. You haven't given anyone three days in a long, long time."

"I haven't given anyone *any* days in a long, long time," Julia corrected, as she neatly folded the items, then pulled on her jeans.

"Not since Dillon."

"Yep, not since Dillon," she said, turning away because she didn't want McKenna to see how much it hurt to even hear that name breathed. Dillon was the reason she kept secrets from her sister, and from everyone. She shifted gears to her sister's upcoming wedding. "Hey, when are we going for your next dress fitting?"

"When you get back from New York, and we can pick your Maid of Honor dress too," McKenna said in a voice laced with true happiness. She'd found her match, and her happily ever after was in her hands. Julia wasn't jealous, not one bit. She was glad for her sister, even though the notion of a happy ending seemed about as far away to her as living on the moon.

* * *

Cubic Z was buzzing at happy hour. Thursday night was one of the busiest of the week, drawing in the one-more-day-till-the-weekend crowds of twenty-somethings as they spilled out of their nearby offices here in the SoMa district of San Francisco. Finance and tech guys and gals abounded, ordering up micro-brews or fancy cocktails.

As Julia mixed a vodka tonic, she turned to her partner-in-crime, Kim. The petite brunette behind the bar was pouring a Raspberry Ale from the tap while absently running a palm across her round belly. She was due in a few months, the first baby for Kim and her husband.

"You're all set to run this place solo for the week-end?" Julia asked.

Kim rolled her eyes and shot her a look as if to say she were being ridiculous. "I run this place when you're not here. I know what to do. Besides, Craig is going to help me out," she said, as she handed the glass to a regular customer, a skinny guy who always stopped by after work. Kim and Julia were both part owners of Cubic Z; they'd bought an ownership stake a year ago, so they served drinks and made sure drinks served the bottom line. Kim's husband had just finished bartending school but hadn't nabbed a job yet and they didn't need an extra bartender at Cubic Z, so she was the sole source of support for the two of them.

"I know. I just wanted to make sure. What can I say? I'm looking out for you and the baby already," Julia said, as she slid the vodka concoction to a customer.

"Yeah, protect us from all the unsavory types," Kim joked, because Cubic Z was upscale, and might draw hipsters who hit on bartenders but didn't attract that sort of more dangerous clientele. "Like that guy," she said, lowering her voice to a whisper as she tipped her forehead to the door. A man stood with his back to them, talking to a friend, a shock of white in his dark hair. Tension knit itself tightly inside Julia, shooting cold through her bones. She didn't want Skunk anywhere near her bar. He'd been here once, and once had been enough. He'd parked himself in a bar stool, ordered a drink, and said one thing and one thing only as he nodded, surveying the joint, "Yeah, I like this place. I like it a lot. You give good pour."

But when the man swiveled around, he wasn't Skunk. He wasn't anyone Julia knew. And there wasn't a reason for her veins to feel like ice. She shrugged it off, the worry that tried to trip her up now and then, the fear that Charlie or Skunk would hurt her or someone she cared about. They hadn't yet. But they could in a heartbeat.

CHAPTER TWO

Clay finished off the rest of his scotch, then glanced at his watch.

"Got someplace to be?" Michele asked.

Damn. He was caught checking the time again, a bad habit he'd started since he invited Julia to join him in New York this weekend. It was nearing ten, and he should cut out of this bar and head home. She'd be arriving tomorrow, and tomorrow evening couldn't come fast enough.

"Yeah. Bed," he said dryly. Michele was his best friend Davis's sister, and his friend too. The three of them had known each other since college. She was one year younger, but had followed in her brother's footsteps, attending the same university.

"I remember when you used to be out till all hours," Michele teased, shooting him a knowing smile as she ran her fingers through her dark hair. She was a pretty woman, always had been, but there was noth-

ing between them. Not since they'd shared a kiss one
night at a drunken college party. A kiss that had never
been repeated, and he'd chalked it up to her being sad
that night over the anniversary of her parents' death
and needing some kind of connection. Understandable. Completely understandable.

"Hardly," he said, because he wasn't the party-boy
type, but then he wasn't usually the first one to leave
either. Tonight, however, needed to end early, because
tomorrow was the evening he wanted to last all night
long. He called for the check, fished some bills from
his wallet, and paid for their drinks.

"Why are you leaving so soon?"

"Because the glass is empty. I'll get you a cab," he
said, and walked out with her, the neon lights of the
diner across the street flickering behind them. "Do
you want to . . ." she said, but the rest of her words
were swallowed by the sound of a siren a few blocks
over.

"Want to what?" he asked when the noise faded.

She swallowed, and then spoke quickly, faster than
usual. "Do something this weekend? Have dinner,
maybe?"

He shot her a look like she wasn't making sense as
he hailed the first taxi he saw. "Davis is out of town,"
he said. He and Michele didn't have dinner together.
Drinks, definitely. But dinners were something the
three of them did together, and Davis was off in Lon-

don for a few months, directing a production of *Twelfth Night* that Clay had hooked him up with.

"Yeah. I know," she said. "That's sort of the point."

"Point of what?"

She shook her head. Rolled her eyes. "Nothing. It was nothing," she said, and something about her tone seemed clipped.

"You okay?"

She nodded quickly. Too quickly. "I'm great," she said, as he held open the cab door for her. "Anyway, you probably have big plans this weekend."

"I think it's safe to say I'll be tied up," he said, though as her cab sped off, he realized it was more likely the other way around. That Julia would be.

He hoped she would be, at least.

* * *

He'd woken up at four-thirty, worked out at five, and hit the office by six-thirty. He'd skipped lunch, ordered in a sandwich, and reviewed a contract for a new sci-fi flick a movie director he repped was working on. He sent in notes to the producers, a list of points and items that needed to be changed. If they weren't, his client wouldn't be happy, and Clay was all about having a hefty stable full of happy clients.

His junior partner at the firm, Flynn, poked his head in around mid-afternoon. "Hey. I got a lead that the Pinkertons are looking for new representation," Flynn said, his blue eyes wide and grinning. A pair of

British brothers, the Pinkertons had been bankrolling some of the most successful films in the last few years, including *Escorted Lives*, based on the best-selling books.

"We need to lock that up," he said, and he was sure the glint in his eyes matched Flynn's. Three years younger and eager as hell to grow his role at the firm, Clay had hired him fresh out of law school. Flynn had become invaluable, pulling more than his weight in helping to land top clients and sweet deals for them. They'd seen eye to eye on just about everything, with the exception of one minor rough patch a year ago over a client that Flynn had reeled in all on his own—a big-time action film director.

A client they'd lost.

"No kidding," Flynn said, tapping the side of the door twice for good luck. Flynn was like that, always crossing his fingers, and knocking on wood. "I'll get some more details and aim to set up a meeting with them next week."

"Perfect. The Pinkertons are huge golfers, so if you have to schedule a tee time, you should," he said, and it wasn't so much a suggestion as it was an order, and one he knew Flynn, a former college golfer, would jump at.

Flynn mimed swinging a club. "Shame I hate golf so much."

"All right, get out of here. I need to finish up so I can take the weekend off."

"I'll email you when I hear more."

"I'm not answering email this weekend," Clay said, making it clear in his tone that this was a do-not-disturb kind of weekend. "You can update me on Monday."

"Fair enough."

Flynn left, and he checked on Julia's flight, pleased to see it was landing on time. He brushed his teeth, ran his fingers through his hair, not bothering with a comb, because she was the kind of woman who'd have her fingers sliding through his hair in seconds, messing it up the way she wanted. He said goodbye to the receptionist, let her know she could shut down early too, and slid into the town car waiting outside his office. On the way to the airport, he worked his way through his west-coast calls, ending them just as the car pulled up to the terminal.

The sun was blaring high in the sky in April, so he put on a pair of sunglasses. He loosened his tie; he couldn't stand the way it constrained him. He glanced at his phone, hoping for a message from her. None was there, so he clicked on the app for his stocks, checking his portfolio, and looking up every few seconds to scan the crowds. He couldn't focus on the market right now.

He hardly wanted to admit it to himself, but there was something about this moment—the minutes before he saw her—that felt like first-date nerves. Like knocking on a woman's door, and waiting, hoping she'd be just as eager for the night to unfold. Weird, considering the way he and Julia had started. Free of pretense and bullshit, they went straight for each other, the physical chemistry overpowering anything else.

His phone buzzed. He clicked open the message and it sent a bolt of electricity through him. *White stockings coming your way . . .*

Stockings—one of those items of clothing that on the right woman could send a man to his knees. Especially the sight of the top of a pair of thigh-highs peeking out from a skirt, revealing an inch of skin, hinting at what lay beneath. On Julia, stockings were a playground for his eager hands.

The nerves in him disappeared and turned into something else—adrenaline, maybe. The sharp, hot charge of desire all through his blood and bones.

He spotted her before she saw him; that red hair was hard to miss, even in a sea of frenzied, frantic travelers jostling for a cab, a car, a bus. She wore a black trench coat, belted at the waist, black heels, and white stockings. A grin took over his face; she had done it. Of course she had done it. He was at attention in seconds and his fingers itched to touch her, to peel off those stockings inch by delicious inch, then lick his way down her legs to her ankles and back up, savoring her every single second.

Leaning against the town car, he kept his eyes on her the entire time as she threaded her way through the crowds. She was a tall drink of woman, her red lipstick matching her red hair that was blowing in the late afternoon breeze. She brushed some strands away from her face. Soon, she noticed him, and smiled wickedly. He nodded, trying to act cool, even as his temperature rose. Then, she was in front of him, and before she said a word, her hands were on his shirt and she pulled him to her, pressing her lips to his.

She was lightning fast. A blur of movement, of teeth and lips, and that intoxicating taste of her lipstick that would be gone in seconds.

He responded instantly, kissing her hard like she deserved. Cupping the back of her neck, he jerked her close. He wanted her to remember that she might have made the first move, but he liked to lead. He nipped on her bottom lip then sucked on her tongue, drawing out a moan from her that pleased him deeply. He kissed more, sliding his tongue over hers as he lowered his hand to her thigh, skimming his fingers along the thin, barely-there fabric of her stockings.

When he broke the kiss, he raised an eyebrow. "They look good on you, and I bet they look good coming off too."

"Don't rush it. I want you to enjoy the view."

"I've been enjoying the view since the second I laid eyes on you, gorgeous."

He opened the door and gestured for her to enter the car, watching the whole time as she stepped inside and crossed her legs, giving him a very brief preview of where the stockings ended. He shook his head approvingly, and she shot him a look that said nothing short of *come and get it.* He took her suitcase as the driver emerged, scrambling to deposit the black carry-on into the trunk.

After he got in the car he hit the partition button, closing them off from the driver, with the tinted windows shutting them off from the whole wide world.

She looked at him, her pretty green eyes meeting him straight on. That beautiful face, that divine body, and that naughty, naughty mouth; it was hard to believe he'd only spent one night with her. She stared at him as if she was as famished as he was. As if she needed the same thing.

"You look like you need to be fucked right now."

"Do I?"

"You sure do," he said, raking his eyes over her, perched in the leather seat so properly, and so damn sexily at the same time. He ached to touch her but savored the tease, so he kept a distance between them, drawing out the tension as the car pulled into afternoon traffic.

"And I suppose you think you can solve that problem?"

"I don't think so. I know so. And I intend to. But not yet."

"You gonna toy with me?"

"Been thinking about it."

"Like a cat playing with a mouse," she said, her voice nearly a purr.

"You're hardly a mouse."

"I know," she said, and ran her index finger across her bottom lip then around to her top, so suggestively he nearly tossed his plans to wait out the window. He wanted her now. He wanted her bad, especially with the way her hot gaze was locked on him as she parted her lips, and ran her tongue along her teeth.

A challenge; one that he planned to meet. A low rumble worked its way free of his throat as he moved to her, his body next to her, just a trace of contact. Slowly, so as to torture her, he reached for the belt of her coat, taking his time untying it.

Her breath caught as he started to open her jacket, first one button, then the next, then another. As he worked his way up her chest, undoing the final button, she rolled her eyes in pleasure, closing them briefly as he slid a hand over her right breast, squeezing her.

She stifled a gasp, biting her lip.

"Don't pretend you're not turned on."

"I'm not pretending," she whispered.

"Then let me hear you moan. I want to hear everything." She opened her eyes, as he cupped her breasts over the fabric of her clingy sweater. "Are you wet?"

"Yes."

He glanced down at her short black skirt, already rising up to show more of her strong, shapely thighs.

He desperately wanted to slide his hand under her skirt right-the-fuck now, but patience would be rewarded. "When did you start getting wet?"

"The exact moment?"

"Yes."

"On the plane."

"What were you thinking about at thirty thousand feet that was getting you wet?" he asked as his hand drifted down the front of her sweater, traveling over her flat belly.

"About all the things you might say to me."

"You like the way I talk to you?"

"Why don't you check and see how much I like it?"

"Why don't you wait for me to check," he fired back as he reached under her sweater, spreading his hand across the soft, sweet flesh of her stomach. She moaned as he touched her, and he wasn't sure he was going to be able to get enough of those sounds this weekend. He might have to spend the next forty-eight hours making her gasp and moan, groan and scream, because her noises were better than a cold drink on a hot day. The sounds she made fed him.

He ran his callused fingers along the waistband of her skirt, and she wiggled closer to his hand. "So your panties were damp all during the flight, Julia?"

"I wouldn't say the whole flight. I have control, you know," she said, shooting him that tough stare that turned him on even more.

"I know you do. You have excellent control. And I love breaking it down. I love watching you lose control," he said, dipping his hand inside her skirt. "So tell me what you thought about on the plane that aroused you."

"Your mouth," she said in a rough whisper.

"Nice answer." He trailed his fingers along the top of her panties, and her hips arched closer.

"Got any other questions for me?"

He nodded. "Did you get wetter when you saw me? Tell me the truth," he said, pulling his hand out of her skirt. She looked up at him, wide eyes full of need.

"What do you think?" She reached for his hand, locking fingers with him. She tried to tug his hand down to her legs, but he didn't budge.

"I think you're as hot between your legs as I am hard just from looking at you," he said and brought her hand to his erection, letting her press her palm against him. She grinned as she touched him, stroking him. He hissed in a breath, but then moved her hand away. "So tell me. Did I make you wetter when you saw me?"

"Yes. You leaning against the car, with that tie all loosened and your jacket on, looking like a hot guy in a suit. Only I knew you weren't thinking of business deals—you were thinking of bedroom deals."

"I was watching you the whole time, getting harder as you walked toward me. Seeing you wore what I told you to wear," he said, teasing the top of her lacy stockings. He could feel her heat without even touching her. He bent his head to her neck, flicking his tongue against her collarbone, then up to her ear. "Tell me one word to describe how wet you are now."

"What is this? Mad Libs foreplay?" she said in as challenging a tone as she could likely muster. He was impressed with her fierceness. She didn't give it up easily, even as her body was melting under his touch. He traveled higher with his fingers, inching closer to the Promised Land.

"Yes it is. Now, I want one word," he said firmly, giving her a clear command. He stroked the soft skin of her inner thigh, causing her to quiver.

"Soaked," she said, breathing hard.

"No, your panties are soaked. I want to know about your pussy. One word about your beautiful pussy that I have been thinking about all week long."

"*Slippery.* Does that work for your little wordplay, Clay?"

"It does," he said. Did anyone else on the plane know you were so turned on?"

She shook her head.

"Good. Because I fucking love the image I have in my head now. You flying high above the country, your sexy legs crossed, trying to hold in how much you wanted me to touch you. Not being able to touch yourself, but wanting to so badly. Did you want to masturbate on the plane?"

"No. I wanted you to touch me. I was waiting for you to touch me."

"I'm not going to make you wait any longer."

She grabbed his arm, wrapping her hand around his bicep, sending him some kind of message with the sharp nails that dug into him, right where she remembered his tattoo to be. "You better not make me wait any longer."

He dragged one finger against the cotton panel of her panties, and a growl erupted from him: a long, slow, appreciative growl. Her breathing grew harder, nearing a pant as he stroked her.

"I was wrong," he said in a low voice.

"About what?"

"You are fucking soaked, and I can't let you sit like this. I can't let this delicious wetness go to waste," he said, reaching under her skirt with both hands, and tugging her panties down past her knees. He stopped at her ankles, and she arched an eyebrow in question.

"The panties stay here. I want to hold your ankles in place."

"You weren't kidding when you told me what was on the menu this weekend," she said, her lips curving up in a delicious grin.

"I take my restraints very seriously," he said, twisting her panties in his hand, tightening the hold on her feet.

Keeping the underwear in place, he ran his fingers across her sweet, slippery pussy, watching her mouth fall open, and her eyes drift closed. "It would be so wrong of me to just finger you," he mused playfully as he coated his fingers in her wetness.

"Are you going to fuck me then?" Her voice was so desperate, her body so in need of what he planned to give her.

"I'm going to fuck you with my tongue," he said, letting go of the scrap of fabric to grab her hips and slide her down onto the seat. He spread her open as he pushed his leg down hard on her panties to keep her high-heeled feet bound together. He was ready, *so* ready to taste his woman. "The last time I did this to you, I tied you up, Julia. But this time I want your hands free to grab my face, pull hard on my hair, do whatever you need to do. You can fuck my face hard. When I get out of this car, I want to look like a man who was eating pussy."

"Oh God," she gasped as her head fell back against the seat.

He buried his face between her legs, and she cried out. A loud, no-holds-barred yell that echoed off the windows of the car, it was the most beautiful sound in the world. She gripped his head with her strong thighs, an involuntary reaction to the first touch as he licked her. Then she let her knees fall open for him and he savored her, working her up and down with his tongue, his lips, his mouth. He lapped up all her juices, the taste of her intoxicating and making his cock even harder, if that were possible.

He drove his tongue inside her, setting off another shattering moan that was music to his ears. She was quite an instrument to play, so finely tuned, and if he touched her right, she made the most glorious sounds —raw, intense, absolutely delicious noises of pleasure as he plundered her with his tongue. She grabbed his hair, yanked and pulled him closer as he'd told her to do. She started rocking her hips against his face, her exquisite pussy rubbing all over his stubbled jaw. She moved faster, and harder, and she was fucking him furiously right now, taking charge of how she liked it, her breathing turning wildly erratic, her moans signaling how close she was to release. He thrust one finger inside her, crooking it and hitting her in the spot that turned her moans into one long, high-pitched orgasm. She shuddered against him, her legs quaking, and when he finally slowed to look up at her, he saw her hair was a wild tumble, and her face was glowing.

He watched her reactions, enjoying the way the aftershocks seemed to radiate through her body like waves. He moved to the seat, slid alongside her, and pulled her close, tucking her sexy body against his.

"Forgive my manners. I didn't even ask how your flight was."

"It was worth it, Clay. My flight was worth it."

CHAPTER THREE

They barely made it inside his apartment. Before the door even closed, he'd hiked up her skirt. Were they on the fourth floor? Or the fifth floor? Hell, if she knew. Hell if she cared.

She grappled with the zipper on his pants, tugging and pulling as he caged her in against the wall with his strong arms. She pushed his pants down, then his briefs, and she wrapped an eager hand around his cock, hot and throbbing in her palm. He drew a sharp breath at the first touch, and she loved this; the moment when a man was helpless to her touch. When the control all swung back to her.

They were so simple, men. When it came down to it, they were ruled by their erections. Even when she gave in to a man, she still knew who was always in charge. She was; the woman was. Especially as she watched the expression on his gorgeous face, his eyes rolling back in his head as she stroked him. He rocked into her fist, fucking her hand once, twice, three times.

She dipped her free hand into her sweater, then inside the cup of her bra, hunting out the condom she'd stowed there earlier. You never could be too safe or too ready, she'd reasoned.

She ripped open the foil, and the sound make his eyes snap open.

"You come prepared," he said.

"I prepare for coming," she replied, then rolled the condom on him, loving the way he watched her hands as they slid down his length..

"Now, fuck me against the wall, Clay. Fuck me hard and fast, and if you think I can't take it, fuck harder then," she said.

"You think you give the orders here? I'm going to make you pay for that later," he said, as he grabbed her ass, hitched her legs around his waist and sank into her.

Her mouth fell open into an *O* as he filled her, his long, thick cock buried deep inside her. He didn't move for a few seconds, giving her time to adjust to his size even though she didn't need to. She loved how he stretched her, how she could feel him deep and far inside.

He began thrusting, his strong hands gripping her flesh, his fingers digging into her cheeks. She was the helpless one now, immobile, pinned by the wall and his big, sturdy body, but she reveled in it. Her mind was blank, free of nothing but this moment, this pure, physical, hungry moment with this man.

"How are you going to make me pay for it?" she asked, her words coming out choppy with each hard thrust inside her.

"By teasing you later. By tying you up and bringing you close to the edge, and then stopping right before you come," he said, his voice a low dirty growl, his breath hot against her neck.

"No," she moaned. "That's not fair. I don't like teasing."

"I know you don't. And I don't like being told to fuck you hard," he said, slowing his moves to drive as deep as he possibly could in her, making her breath catch in her throat. "You think I'd do anything but fuck you hard when I have been waiting all week for this?"

"All week? You've been waiting all week?"

He dipped his head to the crook of her neck, planting a bruising kiss on her skin as he slammed into her once more, his cock rubbing her clit and filling her at the same delirious time. She moaned loudly, so loud she was sure the next street over heard her, and she didn't care one bit. He was fucking her worries away, and the harder he took her, the less she cared about the way she spent her Tuesday nights.

"Yes. All. Week. Long," he said, punctuating each word with a thrust. "I've been picturing your legs wrapped around me, your hot body against mine, and most of all, I've been thinking about making you come again. I want you to scream, Julia. I want to feel the way you grip my cock when you come on me," he said, in that rough, sexy voice that sent sparks tearing through her body.

"Me too, Clay. Me too," she whispered, letting go of the game, of the banter, of the way they teased each other because right now, she was starting to see stars, beautiful, silvery stars, as the world slipped away, and he filled her, taking charge of her body, sending her over the edge. Her belly tightened. "Oh God," she cried out.

"Yeah, just like that. Come for me now, come so fucking hard for me so I can feel you all over," he said, holding onto her as she shattered into the beautiful bliss of another orgasm, the pleasure riding through her, stretching and reaching into the far corners of her body and mind.

Then, as she was catching her breath, she felt her spine scrape the wall as he surged into her once more, the look on his face, the growl in his throat making it clear that he'd joined her, and that they'd come undone together.

* * *

She was willing to admit it. She had apartment envy, and she had it bad. He had not one, but two sets of *stairs*. Which meant he had three floors: the loft level up top, then a living room level in between, then the kitchen and dining-room floor.

She trailed her fingers along the granite counter in his kitchen, lined with dark oak stools. "And this is where you cook all your gourmet meals?" She eyed the gleaming stovetop that looked as if it had never been used.

"You think I don't cook?" Clay handed her a glass of Belvedere, then poured another for himself.

"Do *you* cook?"

"I *can* cook. I don't usually though."

"Why not?"

"Because if I cook, I want to cook for someone," he said. Pots and pans hung on hooks on the exposed brick walls of the kitchen.

"And there's no one to cook for?"

"Not lately," he said, and then gestured to the stairs. "Let me show you the balcony."

They left the kitchen area and he led her up six steps to the sliding glass doors in the living room that opened to a balcony; a gorgeous, drool-worthy balcony.

Her jaw threatened to drop but she knew better than to gawk outwardly. Inside, though, she was ogling the spaciousness. This wasn't one of those New York balconies you had to wedge yourself onto sideways and then lean over to catch a sliver of a view. No, the man had a balcony big enough for hosting a summer barbecue, for throwing a party, for strutting around and doing a dance.

"Yeah, it's not too shabby at all," she said dryly as she peered over the edge of the brick railing, looking down at the cars streaming through the West Village, their taillights streaking six stories below. She drank in the view—it seemed all of New York City was visible from her vantage point, and the city was prettier when you watched it from above, when the noises were muted, and the sidewalk smells weren't invading your nostrils. The distance was a protective layer from the soot and scents and madness. She could see clear across to Broadway as it sliced Manhattan diagonally, then down to Tribeca, and over to the Hudson River, glittering, like a sleek ribbon against the night.

She shivered once; the temperature had dipped some and while it wasn't chilly yet, she was only wearing Clay's white button-down shirt.

"You're cold," he said softly, wrapping his strong arms around her, pulling her close, her back to his naked chest. She glanced down at his bicep, and traced the lines of his ink. *Passion*, he'd told her. That's what his tribal tattoo stood for, and it suited what she knew of him so far.

"Not anymore." She smiled, and leaned her head back to look up at him. He brushed his lips against her forehead, and her heart fluttered. Actually fluttered, like a damn bird trying to escape. She was ready to swat it, but she decided to enjoy the moment instead. "I like your arms around me," she whispered, stripping away her usual sarcasm.

"The feeling is completely mutual," he said, reaching for her hand and sliding his fingers through hers.

"And I also like this view. It's amazing."

"It's not too bad," he said.

She elbowed him playfully. "Not too bad? This is magnificent, and I don't care if that makes me seem all wide-eyed. But it's true. Your apartment is gorgeous," she said. She was a sucker for all the exposed red brick, and the warmth it brought to his place. "It's funny, because I'd have pegged you as having some leather or chrome or steel furniture, all black and white and sleek."

"You are confusing me with someone who has issues with his masculinity," he said, holding her tighter, bending his head to her neck to plant a quick kiss.

"You're saying a man who has black leather and chrome in his apartment is compensating for his small size?"

He laughed, a deep rumbly chuckle. "Don't you think?"

She nodded. She liked that his home was warm and lived in. Yes, it was a man's home, but it wasn't the home of a man who was trying too hard. He even had a few plants on the balcony, and Julia didn't have a green thumb herself, but still, there was something nice about this New York lawyer taking the time to have plants. "I can't stand that whole *I'm a man, I need my place to scream mannish.* It's sort of like driving a red Corvette."

"You might notice I don't have a red Corvette. Nor do I need one."

"You definitely do not need one," she said, trailing her fingers down his chest, between his pecs, and across the ridges of his abs. "And your plants are adorable."

He raised an eyebrow. "Maybe if you behave all night I'll tell you their names."

"You do not name your plants," she said, giving him a serious look.

"You're right." He laced his fingers through hers, guiding her back through the sliding glass doors. "I don't name my plants."

They returned to the living room with its dark-brown sofa, and a sturdy coffee table that boasted a couple of books, some magazines, and a few framed photos. There was a picture of Clay in a tux standing next to another man, a handsome one too.

"Where was that taken?"

"Tony Awards a few ago. That's Davis. He's a friend and a client. That was taken the night he won his first Tony. Bastard has a lot of them. Three now," he said, shaking his head, but clearly proud of the accomplishment.

"And this?" She pointed to a shot of him next to a man who had similar features—square jaw, deep-brown eyes, broad, sturdy shoulders.

"Younger brother, Brent."

"Where's he?" Before he could answer she held up a hand. "Wait. Don't tell me more."

He furrowed his brows. "Why?"

"Because I'm famished."

"And that means you can't talk or listen?"

"It means I am saving that conversation so we can have it over food," she said playfully, as she started to unbutton his shirt.

"You're afraid we're going to run out of things to talk about so you want to make sure to hoard a topic for food?"

She wagged a finger at him. "No. I simply want to eat. Now, are you going to cook for me or take me out?"

"There's this thing called takeout. Want Chinese?"

She flinched inside at the mention. The last thing in the world she wanted was Chinese food. She hated that Charlie and his games had ruined that cuisine for her. Sometimes, she just wanted a carton of cold sesame noodles, but they reminded her of all the bullshit she still had to deal with till she was even with Charlie. *If* she'd ever be even with that fucker. Some days, freedom felt a lifetime away. Charlie had her in chains, and even though she hadn't asked for his permission to go away for the weekend, he knew she was gone. She was keenly aware that this was only a temporary leave from the jail she was in back home.

The jail no one knew about. She refused to tell a soul—it was too shameful what had happened that made Charlie turn her into his property. But she also kept her mouth shut because she didn't want those men to sink their claws into the people she loved. She protected her sister, her friends, even her hairdresser with her silence.

But she didn't want Charlie infecting her time away. She shoved all thoughts of debts and guns and knives back into a dark corner of her mind.

"Clay," she said, in a chiding tone. "I can get good Chinese like that—" She snapped her fingers "—in San Francisco. I want something that tastes like New York." The lie rolled off her tongue seamlessly, but he didn't need to know why she wasn't taking him up on his offer for Chinese. "I want to go out. To some place filled with brooding New Yorkers rather than San Francisco hipsters. Something that makes me feel like I'm in the West Village."

"My mistake. I assumed you getting naked meant you wanted to eat in," he said, eyeing her up and down as she unbuttoned the shirt.

"I'm not getting naked," she said. "I'm changing into my clothes."

He reached for her, gripping her wrist in his hand. "Don't."

"Don't change?"

He shook his head. "Wear my shirt."

"I don't even have a bra on," she pointed out, as if his idea was ludicrous.

"I know," he said, his lips curving up. "I like that."

"You like me all free-range?"

"You have beautiful breasts. I want to be tortured knowing they are just one layer away from me, and covered only by something I was wearing an hour ago," he said, trailing his fingers along the edge of the shirt, barely touching her exposed chest. A shiver ran down her spine.

"And what about my bottom half? You want me to strut around naked from the waist down?"

"I want you to put that skirt back on. Do not put on underwear. Just your heels, your skirt and my shirt," he said in a firm voice. He held her gaze, his eyes darker than usual, waiting for her answer.

"Are you giving me an order?" she asked, pushing her fingers through her hair that was still messy from sex. But she'd never minded sex hair. As far as she was concerned, it was a look that should be listed on the menu at all blowout salons. *Updo, blown straight, or sex hair? I'll take the sex hair, thank you very much.*

"I'm giving you a request. One that I very much want you to fulfill," he said, grabbing her hand and bringing her palm to his lips. He kissed her, his tongue soft and wet against her skin. She'd never expected being kissed on her palm would be so erotic, but it was, because everything about Clay was charged with his smoldering virility, like a trailing scent of lingering sexiness that surrounded him. She was familiar with the term "sex-on-a-stick," but that didn't even begin to describe this man. He was so much more than that. He was masterful, and he touched her in ways that felt unreal. As if it weren't possible to truly feel that good. But, this was no mere dream. It was an intoxicating sliver of reality.

"What if I want to wear underwear?" she said, challenging him because it was fun, because she could, and because he wasn't going to pull a knife on her if she did. Here, she could be herself without fear of retaliation with a weapon. What a relief that was.

"Then I will take it off at the table. So as far as I can see, you can leave your panties here, or I can remove them from you at the restaurant. That clear?"

She nodded. "Commando it is then. And I am going to make you so crazy with wanting me that you might regret telling me to go naked."

"Impossible. I'd never regret you naked."

On the way out, she grabbed her clutch purse—a sleek little number from Coach that she'd snagged second-hand—and her phone. The message light flashed.

"Damn," she muttered, when she saw the text from McKenna. *Are you alive??? Or are you otherwise occupied? I need to know if I should call the cops or congratulate you.*

Julia grinned at the note. Clay raised his eyebrows in question.

"My sister," she explained, tapping a quick reply. "I told her I'd text her when I landed. She worries about me."

"So much that it brings out that naughty grin on your face?" he asked, swiping his thumb across her lips, and it was both sexy, but also skeptical. As if he didn't quite believe her.

But this time she was telling the truth.

CHAPTER FOUR

The Red Line gave new meaning to the word *Lilliputian.* The restaurant was one long narrow hallway, as if it had been wedged in between the shops on each side. There was a long bar, and a few tables, and they sat at the far end near the restrooms. Clay had been here a few times; it was a popular neighborhood place on a cobblestoned street in the Village, and typified what he loved about this eclectic neighborhood—it was thoroughly New York, but it had an individual feel to it, from the black-and-white pictures of steam engines on the walls, to the dark-red counter, to the hip-hop playing faintly overhead, R. Kelly's "Ignition."

Julia had finished texting with her sister, and he was glad of that. He had nothing against cell phones, but the sight of one in a woman's hands while he was with her didn't sit well with him, and he had his ex, Sabrina, to thank for that. She'd kept her twitchy little fingers far too busy on the touch screen of her phone, then lied, lied and lied some more about what she'd been doing. She'd been involved in some bad shit, and had dragged him deep down into her troubles, too. It had taken him longer than he'd wanted to untangle himself from those tall tales Sabrina had spun, and the damage she'd done to him. Since then, he'd vowed to stay away from that kind of woman.

Julia's phone was tucked away in her purse again, where it belonged. They'd placed their order and she was nibbling on appetizers. She plucked an olive from a small plate, bit it away from the seed sexily, and then said, "Do you realize I don't even know where you're from?"

"Do you want to know where I'm from?"

"Obviously. I want to get to know you better. Much better," she said.

"And I want you to get to know me much better. Where do you think I'm from?" he asked, taking a drink of his scotch.

"Chicago."

He shook his head. "Try again."

"Ooh. Is this another game? You like games, don't you? First Mad Libs. Now I get to guess where you're from. What do I win if I'm right?"

He leaned in close to her, swept her hair from her ear, and spoke in a low rumble. "You can pick the next position. But I know you won't win."

"So you're saying you're setting me up to fail so you can choose how to take me?"

"You think I'd choose badly? You think I'd pick a position you wouldn't like?"

She shook her head. "No," she said softly, and she seemed to let down her guard for a second or two. "I like everything you do."

He couldn't resist her, especially not when she dropped the snark, though he loved that about her too. But when she revealed her vulnerable side, he found himself wanting to be even closer to her.

"I like doing everything to you," he said, looking her in the eyes then brushing his thumb gently over her cheek before he kissed her softly, drawing out the sexiest little whimper from her gorgeous lips.

She reached for his collar gently, holding on as she kissed back, and it was a kiss that held the promise of so much more. So much of their contact was hard and rough, and they both liked it that way, but this was tender and sweet, and he wanted this side of her too. Judging from how she kissed him, she wanted it too.

Soon, she broke the kiss, and brushed one hand against the other in a most business-like gesture. "Now that that's settled, let the games begin." She studied his face curiously. "California?" She shook her head before he could answer. "No, you're not happy enough to be from California."

"I'm very happy," he said defensively.

"Sure, but California people smile all the time. There's this thing called sunshine that makes us all dopey and cheerful."

"Then how do we account for your sarcasm, Miss California?"

"I'm an outlier," she said, as a waiter brought them water glasses.

"Water for both of you. And the kitchen is working on your orders. They should be out in about five minutes."

"Thank you very much," Clay said, then returned his attention to the beautiful woman by his side who wore no underwear. "I'm not from California."

"Arizona? Nah. Somehow I don't think they make them so kinky in Arizona."

He couldn't help but smile. "You never know. Arizona could be an incredibly kinky state. There could be entire colonies of kink in Phoenix."

"If there are colonies, perhaps we should go exploring. But no, you're not from Arizona, and you're not from Oregon or Washington either. You'd be crunchy, or have more of a penchant for plaid if either were the case."

"I enjoy your process of elimination," he said, leaning casually back in his bar chair, crossing his arms. No one ever guessed where he was from, because it was the kind of place people weren't usually from.

She pressed her fingers to her lips, then pointed at him. "And you're not from Boston because you don't have an accent, and that's also why you're not from the south. Or Texas, even though you feel very Texas," she said, placing her palm against his shirt, spreading her fingers across his chest, tapping lightly with her fingertips. He was hard instantly from her touch. Damn this woman; everything she did was a direct line to his dick.

"So, is there a guess coming, Julia?"

She shrugged happily, held her hands out in an *I give up* admission. "Salt Lake City," she said with a smirk, and he laughed at her guess, so intentionally wrong.

"Vegas, baby."

Her features registered no reaction at first. She was simply silent. Then she laughed, maybe in disbelief. "No one is from Vegas. Vegas is where you go. Not where you're from."

"Born and raised there."

She held her hand as low to the ground as she could from where she sat. "Like, back when you were little?"

He nodded again. "All the way through high school too. Happy to show you my diploma if you need more verification. Lettered in Varsity Football at Desert Hills High on the outskirts of town. Lived there till I moved east for college."

"And how does one come to live in Vegas?"

"Generally speaking, one has parents from there."

"Clearly. And your parents? What do they do in Vegas?"

"My parents do exactly what you'd expect two people in Vegas to have done. They're retired now. Mom was a showgirl. Dad owns a small casino off the strip."

"Wow. That's just so . . ." she said, then let her voice trail off.

"So what?"

"Unusual. And surprising," she said.

"Why is it surprising?"

* * *

You have got to be kidding me.

Her heart had raced when he'd first said Vegas, but she'd reined it in, relying on her well-honed poker face. Because really, what were the chances that he'd hail from the gambling mecca?

Of all the places he could be from, she'd never have thought it would be the *one* place that had so much in common with her present, and the life of gambling she'd led. She'd been a card player long before her mandatory attendance at Charlie's Tuesday night games. She'd known her way around a deck of cards since she'd taught herself to play in high school, and then continued on during college at UCLA, finding late-night games in the dorms, winning handily most of the time, collecting extra money for her expenses, for textbooks, and meal plans. Back then, playing had been fun, something she enjoyed. She and her sister had taken many girls' trips to Vegas too in their early twenties. McKenna could never back down from a challenge, and even though board and video games were more of her sister's speed, she was the ideal cheerleader when they'd played the tables late at night at the Bellagio.

"Just because you hardly meet anyone from Vegas, that's all I mean," she said, making light of her comment. She wasn't going to tell him more. Not even McKenna knew how much Julia played these days, and how desperately she needed to win. Only her hairdresser had an inkling. It was better that way, safer that way for everyone. McKenna had had a rough go of things for a while with her douchebag of an ex-fiancé, but now that she'd met Chris she was happy beyond measure. Julia wasn't going to ruin her sister's happiness by letting her know about the crap she was dealing with. McKenna would only be worried, like a good big sister.

There was nothing McKenna could do about her debt, so there was no reason to let her know. She *had* to shield her sister from her troubles. If she kept McKenna in the dark, she could better protect her from Charlie's shadow, and any harm he might do. The same went for Charlie; the less he knew about her family, the better. Chris and McKenna both ran successful, high-profile video shows; she didn't want Charlie to get a piece of them. They were precisely the type of meal he enjoyed best—they were flush with green.

"You like Vegas?"

"I do. And I can hold my own at a blackjack table."

"Yeah?"

"Why? You think women can't gamble?"

"Why would I think that? Do I look like a sexist pig?"

"No," she said with a laugh, and held up her hands in surrender. "Do you play?"

He nodded. "I play poker a couple times a month. One of my lawyer buddies has a regular card-game going on. A few of my clients play."

"Do you let them win?"

He laughed, and shook his head. "Never. They'd know if I were letting them beat me. Besides, they're A-list actors and producers."

"Name dropper," she said, bumping her shoulder against his.

"Did I say their names?" he tossed back. "Anyway, they don't give a shit how much they win or lose."

"Nobody likes losing," she said, trying to keep the sharp edge from her voice. She despised losing because it kept her chained to that man, tied even longer to a debt that wasn't hers. Nobody could shrug off losing. But then, what did she know? She didn't have tons to gamble with, so she hated losing even more.

"True, but we all just play for fun. Nothing more, nothing less. Couple guys, smoking cigars, talking shit, and laying down some bets. My second-favorite pastime," he said, raising an eyebrow.

She flashed him a naughty grin, but inside, a sliver of envy wedged itself in her heart. She wanted to love the game, and part of her still did. But that part was crushed like an old cardboard box by the weight of all that she owed. Charlie had subverted both her skill and her love of poker into something dirty, making her his ringer to take down poker babies. Someday she'd like to play again for fun. Hell, maybe she could even tolerate losing if she didn't face the consequences of knives, guns, and threats to her livelihood.

"I know what your first favorite pastime is," she said, trailing her finger along his thigh.

"We could combine the two. You'd be nice to play strip poker with," he added.

"I'd beat you," she said instantly. She knew she would. Confidence coursed through her.

"I'd have to say in that game with you, I'm winning either way."

"You're an interesting man, Clay Nichols," she said, smiling at him. But smiling inside, too. She was enjoying herself so much, and so much more than she had in ages. There was something about him that simply worked extraordinarily well with her. They had chemistry in the bedroom in spades, but they could talk, too, and that was a magical thing. Rare, too. You didn't often come across someone who captivated your mind and your body. "I want to know more about you. So, you have a little brother. Where does he live?"

"Ah, the topic you were saving for dinner. Brent is in Vegas too."

"Wait. Let me guess." She flung her hand over her forehead, mimicking a fortuneteller. "He's a magician. He has an act with tigers and disappearing roses."

He shook his head. "Nope. But you're close in that he's on stage. He's a comedian."

She shook her head, bemused with his family story. "Your family does all the things you never really think anyone does."

"And we have Thanksgiving together every year, too. Mom makes a turkey, Dad carves it, and Brent bakes a pumpkin pie."

"Oh, stop. That's far too normal to be believed. Aren't you supposed to have issues? Like everyone these days? Hate your dad or mom? Or something," she said because her ex, Dillon, certainly was like that. Most of the men she'd known were prickly toward their families and, come to think of it, that might be yet another reason why they were exes. Shouldn't a man have a little respect for his mom and dad? There was no badge of honor given for hating your parents simply because that's what most modern men and women did.

"What can I say?" He held out his hands in mock surrender. "I aim to defy modern stereotypes. I might have grown up around gamblers, tits and ass, but there was no drama. No dysfunction. Why? Were you thinking I had some horrible childhood, and that's why I like to talk dirty to you?"

She pressed her finger against her lips, and peered at the ceiling as if in deep thought. "Actually, I kind of figured you were the same as me, and that you just liked it that way."

"Damn straight. I'm not playing out some childhood trauma in the way I like to have sex," he said in that smooth, confident voice she loved.

"Sometimes a cigar is just a cigar."

"You'd look sexy smoking a cigar. But then you'd look sexy in just about anything. Which is sort of my point. I like what I like, and I like it all with you."

A shiver raced through her blood at his words. She brushed her lips against his jaw. "I feel the same about you," she whispered, and he took her in his arms quickly, a warm, strong embrace. He didn't say anything, just breathed her in, and she did the same. The moment felt suspended almost, existing in its own blissful bubble of possibility. Her mind toyed with the potential of the two of them, of the ways this moment could turn into many more. She liked being with him so much, maybe too much.

"What's your story?" he asked after she slipped slowly from his hold. "Do you bake pumpkin pie at Thanksgiving?"

"I'm more of a pecan pie kind of gal. And yes, I have one of those—shockers—normal families too. Though not nearly as exciting as yours. Mom's in real estate, Dad's an orthodontist, and they live in Sherman Oaks, California, where I grew up. My best friend is my sister. Well, my other best friend is my hairstylist, Gayle, but then, who else does a woman tell all her secrets to but her hairdresser?" she said playfully.

"I hate secrets," Clay said in a harsh tone with narrowed eyes. His words jolted her, as if she'd been shocked by the unexpected ire in his statement. Julia's gaze drifted down; his fists were clenched.

"What do you mean?"

"Secrets eat away at people," he said, practically spitting out the words on the red counter.

She'd touched some kind of nerve.

CHAPTER FIVE

Okay, fine. She got it—secrets could suck. But she had a big one, and she didn't need or want to feel like she was doing something wrong by keeping it. She had no choice. She was boxed in by her awful ex and what he'd done to her, and now by what Charlie was doing to her as he made her pay for Dillon's crimes—crimes he blamed on her. Some days she felt like she'd never get out from under it all. Not from Charlie, and not from the need for secrets and lies.

She grabbed the steering wheel of the conversation and swerved out of the way of the topic. "I have a secret I can tell you. Mine is that I'm wearing no underwear."

That earned her a wicked grin. He laid a strong hand on her knee. "Hardly a secret. I knew that. Tell me things that are secret now, but won't be in a few seconds. Tell me what you love most in the world," he said.

"Cupcakes, my sister, and freedom," she said, and truer words were never spoken.

"And what do you hate most?"

That was easy. Too easy. "Being made a fool. Owing things," she said, and because she didn't want to discuss it more she turned the question back on him. "What do you love most in the world?"

"Scotch. Ties. Movies. Family."

"And what do you hate most?"

"Lies. I hate lies."

"But you're a lawyer," she said, furrowing her brow.

"So that means I can't dislike lies?"

"Don't you have to lie for a living?"

"No. I don't have to lie," he said, and his voice was strong and passionate. "I fight. I fight for what my clients want. There's a difference."

"What else do you fight for?"

"For the things I want."

"Do you want me?" she asked, turning the conversation down another street yet again.

"I want you so fucking much, Julia," he said, and he wasn't giving an order or a command this time. There was something almost naked in his voice, a vulnerability that he let show now and then. He pulled her close, buzzed his lips along her jaw, then up to her ear. "I meant it when I said I couldn't stop thinking about you all week. I wanted to fuck you, and I wanted to talk you. I want to spend more time with you. I want to get to know you more and more. You fascinate me," he said, kissing her neck, his sandpaper stubble rough against her skin, the feel of him melting her inside.

His words sent a shudder through her, filling her with that delicious feeling of falling in like with someone. Of flutters and wishes and the hope for more—more time, more moments. But saying she wanted more was hard for her. Letting someone in was even tougher, because she knew where it might lead to—to her being owned in yet another way she'd never see coming. So she shifted back to the pure truth of the physical.

"Now you're turning me on again," she whispered.

"It's a good thing you're not wearing any panties."

"Oh yeah? Why's that?"

He pulled away, glanced around the restaurant as if he were sweeping it for spies, then reached into his back pocket. There were a few other diners at nearby tables, as well as the bartender and the waiter. He took his hand from his pocket, his fingers curled around in a fist, like he was hiding something.

"Are you a good actress?" he asked.

"Sure. Why?"

"Because I'm going to test you right now." He slid his hand under her skirt; her legs were hidden under the edge of the counter. Then she felt it—a buzzing against her bare thigh.

"What is that?" She hitched in her breath.

"Something I got for you," he said. "Do you like coming?"

"Uh, yeah."

"Our dinner will be here any minute," he said, tipping his chin towards the waiter who scurried to the kitchen. "I want you to come before he arrives with the food."

"Clay," she said under her breath, but when he pressed his finger against her center, she bit her lip to silence her groan. The sensation was intense. He had some kind of mini-vibrator strapped to his index finger, and he wasn't messing around. He was hitting her right where she was hot for him, and the sudden friction against her clit turned her insides molten.

"Show me what a good actress you are."

"I'm a great actress," she said, through gritted teeth as he teased the vibrator in a dizzying circle around her flesh. Delicious sensations flooded her body, and she fought her impulse to hold onto the edge of the counter, as he rubbed her faster, sending sparks racing through her bloodstream.

A couple having dinner a few tables away pushed back their chairs, the legs scraping across the wood floor. The man held the woman's coat, and the woman looked in Julia's direction as she slid her arms into the sleeves. Julia plastered on a fake smile, pressing her lips firmly together, shutting inside her mouth all the moans and scream and cries she wanted to unleash.

"I'm looking forward to eating. I hope the food arrives soon," Clay mused, keeping one hand under her skirt as he reached for his scotch with his free hand. He tapped her clit with the vibrator, gently but insistently, sending an exquisite pulse between her legs that spread like ripples, reaching all the way to her fingertips.

Oh God. She wanted to roll her eyes in pleasure, to spread her legs wide.

"What about you, Julia? You hungry for your risotto?" He tilted his head to the side, giving her a deliberately curious stare.

"Sure." She sucked in a moan as a wave of intensity slammed down. She ached with a desperate desire to be touched, to be felt. *To come.* He moved his finger back and forth, the pad of the vibrator driving her into another world of pleasure. Involuntarily, her shoulders curled in.

"You okay?"

"I'm fine," she choked out.

"You sure?" He stroked her fast, then faster. "You don't seem like yourself?"

"Just hungry," she muttered as he pushed harder against her swollen clit, bathing her entire being with the thrilling sensations of vibration. She could barely take it anymore. She'd been reduced to nothing but feelings, the raw physical need for release from the flames lapping up her being. She wanted to throw back her head, run her hands through her hair, slide her palms down her own body to savor every second. But she knew how to bluff. She knew how to fake it.

"I think the food's on its way," he said, gesturing with his eyes to the kitchen door. The waiter appeared, holding it open with his elbow, balancing plates along his arm.

Julia swallowed hard, and wanted to pant, to moan, to scream. She wanted to climb up the walls, to rub herself against Clay's thigh, something, *anything* to relieve the build inside that was teetering on the edge of explosion.

"Looks like he'll be here any second. What about you? You ready?"

"I think I might be," she said in a choppy voice, trying so hard not to give an inch.

But he was hitting her where her body sang, turning her up, all the way on. And if she were alone with him, she'd have grabbed his shoulders and held on hard. Instead, she gripped the edge of the stool, her sharp nails digging into the wood, surely leaving scratch marks as she channeled there all her desires to writhe and moan and let herself bathe in the bliss of the orgasm that rocketed through her body. She was coming, and there was nothing she could do to stop it. The orgasm was on a high-speed chase, tearing around curves, racing through every cell. Julia Bell was coming at the bar, eyes wide open, lips sealed shut, body still as still could be. Every inch of her was lit up and ignited.

The waiter set down their plates as her entire body buzzed with the delicious tingles of an orgasm she hid fiercely.

"Your risotto, miss," he said, gesturing to the plate. Then he set down Clay's meal. "Do you need anything else?"

"I believe I have everything I could possibly want," Clay said, then flashed a quick smile, before turning to her. "What about you? Do you need anything more?"

"I'm good," she said, her eyes bugging out.

"Are you sure?"

"Yes," she said with a satisfied sigh, that one syllable strung out, the only hint of what had just gone down.

The waiter left, and she picked up her fork. "I am famished."

"You deserve some sort of award for that performance."

"My reward will be torturing you when you least expect it."

"I will count down the seconds until that kind of torture comes my way."

CHAPTER SIX

Her phone woke her up in the morning.

She'd turned the damn thing off last night, seeing as she was spent and exhausted from her time with Clay, but now it was buzzing. McKenna probably wanted more details on last night, since they always shared these kind of tidbits with each other—not the nitty-gritty sex details, but the *so you really like him* part. It had been a long time since Julia had actually *liked* someone. With Dillon, the *really like him* feelings had faded well before the relationship ended. Sure, she'd fallen for him in the start, for his self-deprecating humor, for his piercing blue eyes, for the sweet nothings he whispered to her that made her feel special.

She met him when he was one of her students at a weekend class she'd been teaching at a boutique bar in Noe Valley on the art of making cocktails. She'd taken on the class before she bought a stake in Cubic

Z; the class helped supplement her bartending income. And Dillon had been her finest student, his keen eye for detail giving him a leg up as he mixed and matched the perfect amounts.

"You, sir, concocted a most excellent Margarita," she told him.

He'd tapped the side of the glass, and said, "Someday I'll be sipping this in Bora Bora or the Bahamas."

"Wouldn't that be nice? Sitting on a hammock in the sun with a nice cool drink."

"Blue skies and mixed drinks," he added. "A perfect getaway."

One time, after everyone else had left, he'd hung back, raised his hand as if in a classroom, and asked, "I have a question. I know student-teacher relationships are generally forbidden. Does that apply to bartending school, too?"

"Terribly forbidden. Violates all sorts of mixed-drink laws," she teased.

"Call me guilty then," he said, and then asked her out.

They'd gone to a Turkish restaurant in Russian Hill for the first date, then for a walk through that neighborhood. A photographer, he'd made a decent wage shooting interiors of homes in the city for realtors, so he showed her the outside of some of the homes he'd shot, including a rather tiny one that he'd made look palatial in a picture. He used to say that with the right-angled shot he could make any room look "spacious, open and well-lit."

Later, after they became a couple, he was the one who had encouraged her to expand her role at Cubic Z, and to invest in the bar. She didn't regret that decision, not one bit, though she sure as hell regretted him, and wished she'd gotten out sooner.

All his sweetness had leaked away by the end, and they were merely holding on, until he left. The unraveling of that relationship wasn't what hurt; it was the *way* it fell to pieces that stung like snake poison. The way *she* had to bear the brunt of the breakup and all he heaped on her, and she couldn't even tell McKenna the specifics. At times, Julia ached to pour out all the sordid details, especially because her sister understood heartache. But McKenna understood happiness, too. Newly engaged to a man who made her wildly happy, McKenna was in that haze of believing that every new relationship would turn out to be *the one*, so Julia fully expected a text from her sister asking when she'd be getting engaged too.

Ha. *As if* Julia were ever going to do that.

She fumbled for her phone, unlocking the screen. McKenna's name popped up and the first word she saw was *size*. She shook her head in amusement. She wasn't sure if her sister was talking about ring fingers or other measurements, but before she could open the note another text flashed.

Where is the pretty bartender? She wasn't at the bar last night. She should hope she's not skipping town. I wouldn't want to have to inquire with that other woman behind the bar. She seems like she might be preoccupied, and more so in a few months . . .

Her blood ran cold. He'd noticed Kim and her pregnant belly.

She wanted to punch the screen. That slimeball had gone to Cubic Z for one of his pop-ins. Those were the worst, when she had to serve him, and act like she didn't detest him as she poured his martinis. She hoped he hadn't bothered Kim, her hubby, Craig, or anyone else they worked with last night. She didn't want him near her co-workers. She could only imagine how that would go down, especially when Charlie took out his knife and nonchalantly scratched his chin. Those gestures were meant for her—reminders of what he was capable of.

And he was capable of a lot more than just itching a scratch. She'd gotten glimpses of Charlie's cold-blooded nature through Dillon. He'd hinted of things he'd seen while shooting pictures of the limos. Punches thrown, knees whacked, noses broken, eyes blackened . . . Charlie was a man who got what he wanted by any means possible.

Her skin crawled as she imagined him shaking down sweet Kim, the true definition of an innocent bystander.

That was the real rub, though. Everyone in her life was an innocent bystander, and she'd have to keep them innocent. The less anyone knew, the less they could get hurt. If they knew about her troubles they'd try to help her, and then they'd be in his debt somehow, and his crosshairs.

She swallowed back all her anger, and replied quickly. *Of course not. I have the weekend off. Don't worry—I'll be at the game Tuesday, and I plan on winning big again.*

Seconds later, he replied. *That confidence is so alluring.*

She sneered, then her heart beat faster at the next message, from Kim. *You'll be pleased to know there were no unsavory types here last night. Only the usual assortment of hipsters and VCs. So San Fran. Xoxo*

If only Kim knew that there was an unsavory type there last night, scoping them all out. But she planned to be back at the poker table on Tuesday night, working on winning more to line Charlie's pockets, playing hard, and taking down the marks to get out from under his yoke as soon as she possibly good.

She wrote back: *Glad to hear Cubic Z is representing the city so well. Love you madly. See you soon.*

She took a deep breath, reminding herself to push her troubles out of her mind for the weekend. She was far away from all her obligations, and she planned to enjoy her temporary break.

She shut off the phone as Clay stirred. Good—he hadn't seen her texting. He'd seemed perturbed last night when she was writing to McKenna, and she didn't want any weirdness between them. She wanted only good times with Clay, only dessert. This weekend together was the frosting on a scrumptious cupcake. It wasn't real, and that was A-OK. She sure as hell loved a cupcake, and right now she wanted another bite.

Now was as good a time as any to show this man what kind of wake-up call she could deliver, so she slinked down under the sheets and stroked him a few times, enjoying the low rumbles from his chest as he started to wake up.

She wrapped her lips around him, and instantly his hands were tangled in her hair and he held on tight as she licked and caressed him in her mouth. He groaned loudly, and she thrilled at the sound, at knowing she could do this to him, elicit this sort of reaction.

"Good morning to me," he murmured in a sleepy voice. His voice was rough, husky from the early hour, and the sound turned her on even more.

She let him fall from her lips momentarily. "It's going to be a very good morning in a few minutes."

"That's all it's gonna take?"

She arched an eyebrow. "You think I can't make you come quickly?"

"The verdict is out," he said with a lazy grin.

She narrowed her eyes. "For that attitude, Clay, you just bought yourself a wicked tease," she said and returned to his delicious cock, flicking the tip of her tongue up and down his length. He groaned lightly as she licked him, but she stopped short of taking him into her mouth.

"I'm going to take my sweet time now," she said with a purr.

"I can handle it," he said.

"I don't know if you can." She swirled her tongue around the head, then rubbed him against her lips, watching him as she administered her best torture. His chest rose up and down, and his eyes darkened as he stared at her. "It's getting harder, isn't it?"

"It sure is."

"You still want this? I'm not entirely convinced," she said, and blew a stream of air across his cock. He twitched against her lips and she quickly kissed the tip then released him.

He cursed under his breath.

"I didn't hear you. Are you sure you want me to do this?"

"I want you," he muttered, and she grinned, knowing how hard it was for him to have the tables turned.

Still, she wasn't ready to give in. She needed him to want her desperately, to need her terribly. "I think I might require you to ask real nice," she said, as she cupped his balls, lightly rolling them in her hand, then darting down to give a quick lick and kiss to that most sensitive set of parts. She gripped his shaft hard in her hand as she tasted him, and those twin actions set off a long, long moan from Clay.

"Please," he whispered, so low it was barely audible.

"I'm not sure I can hear you," she said, but started giving him his reward, taking him all the way in her mouth, surrounding his hot, hard length with her lips.

He panted hard, and nearly growled at the relief. But she stopped once again, peeking up at him, enjoying the view of his big, strong body stretched out on the sheets. "Do you want it? Ask nicely and I'll give it to you."

He shut his eyes briefly then opened them, holding her gaze. The look was both desperate and hungry. "Please suck me, Julia," he said, in a hoarse voice.

"Gladly," she said, and then gave him the full treatment. First hard, then slow, alternating between teasing him and taking him in.

"Maybe not too long now after all," he said as he gripped her head, sliding his fingers through her hair, tugging as she feasted on him. They kept at it for a bit, him rocking into her mouth, her savoring him all over. He was quieter than usual, though; he wasn't reeling off directions and telling her what to do. Maybe it was because she'd taken the reins. But then his dirty mouth woke up as he pushed her hair off her forehead, looking at her with dark eyes, "Use your teeth."

She slowed for a moment, dragging her teeth lightly against his shaft. "Like that?" she asked, glancing up at him.

The look on his face said it all as his features contorted with pleasure. "Yes. Like that," he rasped out.

"Damn, you like it rough, don't you?" she said, and returned to his cock, touching him exactly how he wanted, scraping gently with her teeth as she moved her lips up and down.

"I like it rough, but I also like pretty much anything you to do my cock," he said, and she took him in further. "Like that," he hissed out. Then she went deeper, drawing out a louder groan from his lips. "And that's fucking good too."

She swirled her tongue around the head as she gripped the base hard in a fist. He hitched in a breath. "That's perfect. Take me all the way in and use those gorgeous teeth, Julia."

Ah, there he was in full force, her dirty-talking, direction-giving man. She smiled, loving the way he used all his talents in the bedroom, his body, his tongue, his cock, and most of all, his *words.* She drew him in, nibbling and sucking and rolling his balls in her hands as he started to fuck her mouth harder, to drive deeper into her.

"You tell me now if I'm fucking you too hard, okay?" he said firmly, but they both knew she wasn't backing down. They both knew she liked it the same way he did. They were perfectly paired in the bedroom; he gave as good as he got, and she did, too. They were two tigers, tussling and tangling and taking each other, talking dirty, playing rough.

"I'm good," she said, even with her mouth full. She dragged her nails along the inside of his strong, muscular thighs, making him shiver, then grazed him right between his legs where his thighs met his cheeks, sending his hips shooting off the bed and deeper into her mouth.

"I love it when you use your hands like that. All over me. I want you all over me, your hands, your tongue. And your lips are so fucking beautiful wrapped around my dick," he said, his narration punctuated by grunts of pleasure. "Fuck, Julia, you're going to make me come so hard in your mouth right now."

She gripped the base with her palm, feeling him twitch hard against her as she sucked him off, his salty, musky taste sliding down her throat as his words started to falter, and his sentences broke into bits and pieces of truncated words. *Feels so fucking good, so good in your mouth,* and then her name, over and over, like a chant. Yes, that was her favorite dirty word that fell from his mouth, when he groaned out *Julia* with unbidden pleasure, and she couldn't help but be satisfied too to have gotten him off so thoroughly, so completely. He looked like a most contented man, a happy grin across his gorgeous face.

"Don't ever doubt me," she said playfully.

"Never." He pulled her up, drawing her next to him, and moved in to plant a kiss on her lips.

She shook her head.

"What? I can't kiss you after I come in your mouth? It doesn't bother me."

"No, that's not it. I just have to confess I hate morning breath, but I really want to kiss you, so how about we brush our teeth and then make out?"

He chuckled deeply, and smacked her ass with a strong hand. "Did I tell you yet how perfect you are? I don't like morning breath either, but then I'm not such an ass that I wouldn't kiss you if you had it." He tapped her nose with his finger. "But you don't."

"Thanks, but there's a toothbrush calling my name anyway."

After they returned to bed with minty-fresh breath, he ran a hand along her hip. "So, what else, besides morning breath? What are your other pet peeves?"

"You really want to know?"

"I really want to know. So I can avoid them," he said, holding her gaze with his own, his dark-brown eyes, so earnest and true, as if it were deeply important for him to know what irked her, so as not to do it.

"Washcloths," she said, and held out her hands as if it say, *what gives*? "I don't get it. I don't understand washcloths. Why use a washcloth to wash your face when you have hands? Put the soap on your hands and wash. Or worse, leaving a wet washcloth hanging up in the shower, because then it just becomes a damp, used, smelly washcloth."

He nodded several times as if taking detailed notes in his head. "You might have noticed I don't own washcloths. I don't need an intermediary between soap and my body."

She laughed. "Exactly. You're already ahead of the game." She looked around the room, as if searching for evidence. "Here's another pet peeve. I don't like seeing a man walking around only in his socks."

He mimed making a check mark. "Note to self: Remove socks first before taking off pants to fuck Julia."

"I don't like dirty sinks either. I see no reason for bathroom sinks to be anything but pristine."

"Did you notice how immaculate my bathroom is?"

"I did," she said with a wink. "Don't you just know the way to a woman's heart?"

"Evidently."

"I assume you were down on your hands and knees scrubbing every surface before I arrived?"

"Something like that. Or maybe I had it cleaned, knowing I was having company I wanted to impress."

She ran her hand along his strong arm over his tattoo. "You're getting the hang of it. You know what to do to stay on my good side."

"Am I on your good side?" he asked, propping himself up on his elbow.

She traced a line down his chest. "You are all good side, Mister. Nothing more."

"Good. How did you sleep?"

"Very well, thank you. You wore me out last night."

"I like wearing you out, Julia," he said, then brushed his lips against her forehead. "And I like having you in my bed."

"Your bed is pretty damn nice."

"You make it look good. I liked having you fall asleep in my arms," he said, then ran his fingers through her hair. He lowered his voice again, speaking softly, "I wouldn't mind seeing you in my bed more often."

There was something different about him in moments like this. Tenderness shined through his hard exterior; a sweetness, even. And it scared the hell out of her. Because it was easy to view him as a weekend fling. So incredibly easy. But when he was like this, she could feel the weight of one word pressing hard on her. *More.*

Like a temptress with a come-hither wave, inviting her in for *more.* More him, more moments, more getting to know each other. She wanted terribly to snuggle in close with him, lift her eyes to meet his, and say, *I want to be in your bed more often, and I want to be in your life, too.*

But she didn't have the luxury of *more.* So she made light of his comment, bringing it down to the sex level. "Oh, you just want to set some sort of record this weekend, don't you?"

"That's not what I meant," he said, and this time his voice was clear, and firm. He pulled her on top of him, threaded his hands slowly through her hair, keeping his eyes locked on her the whole time. "You know that's not what I meant."

"I know," she whispered, the words catching in her throat. She pressed her lips together so she wouldn't say too much, wouldn't admit how much she was starting to want from him.

"Kiss me," he said, giving her a command. She obeyed, exploring his lips with her tongue then crushing her mouth to his, trying to get closer, as close as she could be.

He let go of her hair, his hands drifting down to her backside. He reached for a condom and rolled it on. Then he cupped her cheeks, lifted her up, giving her full access to his erection, and she sank onto him. She inhaled sharply as he filled her, stopping momentarily to savor the sensations. He moved inside her, and it wasn't rough as she rode him. It was luxurious, and deliciously slow, and it felt disturbingly like making love, especially given the way he kissed her tenderly the whole time.

CHAPTER SEVEN

The thieves rode away in a convertible, the sunset streaking behind them, the jewels turned into money and the money tucked safely away in a bank account. The closing credits rolled, and Julia leaned in to whisper in his ear, her soft hair brushing his neck. "We need to stay for the credits."

His heart thumped a beat harder, and he couldn't deny that he was happy she'd insisted on proper movie etiquette herself. He didn't have to tell her he wanted to stay. She got it on her own.

"I always watch the credits, even when I don't have a client involved," he said, staying put in the red upholstered chair because he didn't want to miss seeing the name of the executive producer scroll up the big screen. He'd wait all the way through to the final shot, because that's what you did when you were in the biz. What happens before the credits brings butts to the seats, but what rolls on by after "The End" is why there's a movie in the first place. "But I do have a client in this film."

"Which one is yours?" she whispered as other patrons stood, and picked up emptied popcorn tubs and cartons of Junior Mints.

He pointed to the first credit. "That's my guy."

"And you took good care of him, I trust?"

He nodded. "Got him some very nice points on the back end."

She ran a finger down his arm, giving him an approving nod. "Impressive."

"I do what I can."

The names of the cast and crew, the key grip and the costumer streaked across the screen, and they watched them all. Soon, the movie reached its final frame, and silence filled the theater.

"What did you think of the movie? And don't tell me you liked it because I had a client work on it."

She rolled her eyes. "I have no need to suck up to you, Clay. You're already putting out for me. But I loved it. Especially because you're totally convinced at one point that there's no way they can walk out of the vault with all those jewels, but then it turns out there was a hidden wall," she said, her expression animated as she recounted the film.

He nodded enthusiastically. "That's exactly what I love about a good heist flick. The way the story makes you think one thing, and then all of a sudden," he said, twisting his hand to the side to demonstrate a U-turn, "you've gone the other direction."

"That's what a good story does, right? Surprises you. Challenges you."

The sweeping of a broom interrupted their conversation. Clay glanced behind him. A skinny usher was cleaning the floor of the theater. The thin theater employee dumped the contents of the dustpan into a trashcan and then left.

"I guess that's our cue to go." Clay stood up, holding Julia's hand and they exited their row. "All alone in the movie theater," he mused as they made their way up the aisle. "The things we could do."

"You never stop, do you?"

"Thinking of ways to seduce you?"

She nodded, tucking a strand of her sexy red hair behind her ear.

"Never."

"Your efforts are very much appreciated, but you do know you have this one in the bag?"

He reached his hand around her waist, tugging her in close as they left the theater, the bright lights of the lobby making him blink. "You are not the type of woman I would ever take for granted," he said, whispering low in her ear, because the words were just for her. She shivered lightly against him, and he wrapped his arm tighter around her.

"Why?"

"Why what?"

"Why am I the type of woman you wouldn't take for granted?"

He held open the door to the cinema, letting her walk onto the New York street first, admiring the view of her legs. It was a Saturday afternoon, but she was wearing black stockings and her trench coat. Heels, too. A young man in a slouchy sweatshirt stared at Julia as he walked by, nearly tripping over his Converse sneakers as he craned his neck to gawk. Clay wasn't bothered. In fact, he was a proud motherfucker to know the woman other men stared at was with him. "Because you wear stockings on a Saturday to the movies. Because you do it not just to turn me on, but because you are intrinsically sexy. Because you have this gorgeous internal confidence that has nothing to do with what men think of you. Because you stayed in the theater to watch the credits. Because you *get* why crime flicks are a damn good way to pass two hours. Because as much as I want to spend the entire weekend in bed, I also want to get to know you. Because I like talking to you as much as I like touching you. Is that enough?"

She stopped in the middle of the sidewalk, wrapped her arms around his neck, nodded her answer and planted a hard kiss on his lips. She tasted like kettle corn from the movies.

"Mmm," he growled, as a gray-haired couple sidestepped them. They were in New York City, kissing on the street, doing exactly what new lovers should do on the weekend together.

"Yes, that's enough." She grabbed his hand and laced her slender fingers through his. "And I think you are a fabulous way to pass the time," she said, and he suspected that was as much as she'd admit when it came to that most dangerous territory of *feelings*. But he'd take it; he'd happily take it.

They resumed walking, a crisp April breeze blowing past them that smelled remarkably like rain as they neared Christopher Street. The breeze billowed her coat momentarily, providing him with a full-on view of her long legs, and just the slightest peak of her panties as her skirt danced upwards too. "Because of that, too," he added.

"I arranged for that gust of wind. I ordered it to arrive at this instant."

He laughed, then gestured to a sushi restaurant at the corner. "You hungry?"

She looked at her watch. "It's four in the afternoon."

"I know. But we skipped lunch when I needed to eat you instead, and I figured once we return to my place you're definitely going to be tied up."

"See, here's the thing," she said, holding up her hands, as if offering them for shackling. "You've been promising me these ropes, Clay, and my wrists are still achingly empty."

He swatted her ass. "Get some food in you, woman, before I tie you up and tie you down."

* * *

Clay had been to this restaurant a few times, including once with his ex, Sabrina. She'd asked the sushi chef if she could lick the yellowtail. She wasn't drunk. Sabrina had never been a drinker. She'd been too in love with other substances instead, with little pills prescribed by doctors. "Little darlings for my headaches," she'd say when a migraine swooped down on her. But then the migraines, if she truly had them, became so crushing that she needed those pills more and more.

She needed them all the time. Up her nose. Every few hours.

But the worst part? The way she lied. The times she denied. How she hid what she was up to.

That was the problem. That's also why Clay didn't want any drama with Julia. He knew there were no guarantees in relationships, and certainly people had a way of making and breaking promises. Still, he was keen on this woman, he wanted to spend more time with her, and he wanted to be upfront about the past so they could have more of the present.

After they finished eating and left the restaurant, he cleared his throat. "So, what's your story, Julia? Got any deep dark secrets I should know about?"

She started coughing.

"You okay?"

She nodded, but kept hacking as they passed an art gallery. "Just a tickle in my throat," she choked out.

"Let me go back and get you some water."

She held up her hand to say no, and coughed once more. "I'm fine. But what kind of question is that?"

"An honest question. I'm just trying to get to know you," he said, his tone straightforward.

Then the sky broke, out of nowhere it seemed. The clouds heaved with heavy droplets of water, pelting them from above.

"Holy shit, that's some rain," Julia said, and grabbed at the collar of her coat, as if that would protect her from the water. A few feet away a man hailed a cab, racing to get inside the vehicle. A family down the block ducked into a coffee shop, and a car squealed to a stop at the light.

"We're only three blocks away, but do you want to go to the coffee shop?"

"No. I want to go to your place."

They picked up the pace, Julia's heels clicking loudly against the wet sidewalk. "You okay in those shoes?"

"Totally fine," she said.

"There's a little souvenir shop on the corner. Let me get an umbrella for you."

She grabbed his arm, wrapped her hand around it and pushed him against the brick wall of a shoe store. "Don't even think for a second that I can't handle a few drops of rain, Mister. I'm not some fragile flower."

He held up his hands in mock surrender. "Never said you were."

"I like the rain. And I've always wanted to kiss in the rain," she said, gripping his shirt collar, and running her fingers along it. "Now, give me one of those fabulous New York kisses in the rain that make all the girls swoon."

"Gladly," he said and cupped her cheeks in his hands, held her gaze, then moved in for a kiss, sweeping his lips softly against her, slowly kissing her in the rain, drawing out decadent little sighs and murmurs from her mouth. The sky unleashed a fire hose of water, and the rain became a goddamn downpour. Julia quickly broke the kiss, and pointed to her hair, now plastered against her head. "Okay, time to run because that was romantic for about ten seconds and now I'm just a drowned rat."

He laughed. "Somehow, you're still unbelievably sexy though," he said as he grabbed her hand.

They walked quickly, doing their best to dart and dodge passersby and sprayed-up puddles from cars. He kept his arm around her the whole way, and after another block, they were both soaked, but she couldn't deny that she liked being wet with him, even this kind of wet.

"My coat is useless," Julia shouted against the pounding rain. His jeans stuck to his legs, and her stockings looked waterlogged. Soon enough they reached his building and ran inside. He took a deep breath once the world turned dry again thanks to four walls and a roof.

"That's a hell of an angry sky," he said as they stepped inside the elevator.

"And there's nothing romantic about getting caught in the rain."

He laughed. "Turns out that's all just a lie of the movies." He looked her up and down, her hair clinging messily to her neck, and her cheeks. Her mascara had started to run and a drop of water slipped down her face. "I know what we need."

CHAPTER EIGHT

Candlelight bathed the warm room in its soft glow. A D'Angelo album played faintly from an iPod in the bedroom, but here inside the spacious bathroom with its cream-colored tiles and marble tub, the world was warm again, and the water was the perfect temperature.

Hot.

Julia leaned back against him, her slim body aligning perfectly with his, the waterline bobbing near her breasts. He was sure he could stare at them for quite a while and not ever want to look away. They were gorgeous, full and round, with rosy nipples that he couldn't resist touching. He cupped one in each hand, kneading them.

"Hmm. Where did we leave off? Something about deep dark secrets and skeletons in the closet."

She leaned her head back against him, her hair fanning out in the water like a mermaid's. "Yes. I believe you were going to tell me about yours," she said.

"Ah, so many skeletons," he said, running his index finger across the soft skin of her belly. She sighed happily, snuggling in closer against him.

"I was once a dirty businessman and ran a Ponzi scheme like Bernie Madoff," he said with a straight face.

She turned to look at him. "Really?"

He'd said it so matter-of-factly that it had taken her a moment to realize he was teasing. "No. But the truth is, I ran a high-class call girl ring as a side business to my law practice," he said, in a deliberately confessional tone.

"Shut up." She laughed as she slinked deeper into the water.

"You got me. I never did that. A buddy of mine did, but he got out of that racket recently. Reformed."

"Good. I'm glad to hear that."

"He's the one who runs the poker games I was telling you about. He's also my go-to guy if I ever need to track down intel on someone I'm not so sure about."

"Like an investigator?"

"Sort of. He just knows stuff. He can find out anything about anybody, like that," he said, snapping his fingers. He shifted away from talk of his friend. "But those aren't my skeletons."

"What are yours, then?"

He reached for a bar of soap from the side of the tub, soaped up his hands, and began washing her legs, enjoying the feel of her sexy body sliding across his palms. "Actually, I don't think I have too many skeletons. You know about my family already. I've been a lawyer for ten years; I work hard for my clients, I like entertainment, and I hate lies," he said and she tensed instantly. He briefly wondered why she'd react that way. But then, he reasoned, nobody liked lies. She probably hated them as much as he did. He kept on going, moving from her calves to her thighs. Then he stopped because this was important, what he had to say. "They're a deal breaker for me. There's no need for lies. You agree?"

"Of course," she said quickly.

"I don't like being caught up in something that's a game, or a cheat. Been there, done that. I won't go there again," he said firmly, using his negotiation voice as memories flashed by of his ex. She was the reason he felt this way, and he needed Julia to know he didn't want and wouldn't tolerate a repeat. "I was involved with a woman named Sabrina for a few years. I thought I knew her well, but her whole life was a lie."

"How so?"

"She was addicted to painkillers, and denied it for the longest time. She started taking them for headaches, and she kept on popping more. And she became so wrapped up in it that her life was dictated by it. She missed work, she wrote fake prescriptions, and she started doctor shopping, then selling her stuff to pay for more pills: jewelry, her iPhone, Coach purses . . . anything that had value she sold off to buy more," he said, stopping to gently rinse off the soap from Julia's legs. "I tried to help her. Get her into rehab."

"How did she react to that?"

Clay shrugged heavily, the defeat of those days with Sabrina rising back to the surface. It had been a while since he'd ended things with her for good, and there certainly weren't any residual feelings or lingering love. Still, the memories had a way of wearing him down, because that last year with her had been rough. Her furtive phone calls, the late-night texts to slimy dealers and doctors who started providing for her, and the slide into all those lies. He could still recall the unabated shock he'd felt when he woke up in the middle of the night to find her rooting around in his wallet and pocketing some bills to buy more drugs.

It wasn't even about the money she took. He couldn't care less about the money. It was the lies, and the secrets, and how they both had wore away at him. That last year with her had been the worst twelve months for his firm. The only year his revenues were down from the one before. *Precipitously.* He couldn't concentrate on deals, couldn't focus on clients. The

way she'd toyed with him had nearly cost him the
business he'd worked so hard to build. Flynn had
landed a big client for them—the action film director—
and in the span of those last few months with Sabrina,
Clay had gone and lost that client for them.

If he were a ballplayer, he wouldn't just have been
benched. He'd have been called back down to the
farm leagues for the way he'd messed up that negotiation.

"She was game for it on the surface. Did the whole
contrite act. Said she had a problem and needed help.
But she relapsed every time, and kept going back for
more," he said, and while it had hurt like hell at the
time, it didn't hurt anymore. She was the past, and
he'd learned from it. He wasn't going to repeat those
mistakes again.

Julia laid a gentle hand on his arm, resting it against
the strong, curved strokes of his tattoo. "I'm sorry,
Clay. That sucks."

"Yeah, it did," he said. "It's hard when someone you
care about won't change and won't even try. I kept
trying to help her and she kept promising to get help,"
he said, drawing a circle in the air with his index finger, "but it never happened. And so on you go."

"On you go indeed. And here you are," she said,
twisting around to lay a sweet kiss on his chest. Then
his shoulder. Then up to his jawline.

"Here I am."

"I'm glad you're here with me," she whispered, and it was so unlike her to let go of her hard edge, but he liked it when she did in moments like this. "I'm loving this weekend."

Here he was, falling faster than he expected to.

CHAPTER NINE

That's why he hated lies. Made sense. Made perfect sense. And, hell, she shouldn't worry because she didn't have a drug problem, like his ex had. Not even close. She had a money problem, and it wasn't her fault. But she also had a truth problem, because she couldn't tell a soul about all those dollars she owed Charlie. She certainly couldn't tell Clay. He did well for himself, and she didn't want Charlie to sink his teeth into her new man.

New man?

What the hell? It was one weekend. One moment. Nothing more, and she certainly couldn't think of him as her man, no matter how much she enjoyed every single second of these days with him, from the way he touched her to the way he made her feel in her heart.

Like it could open again.

Like she could let him in and not be burned because there was something about him that simply meshed with her. Maybe it was the way he held her, or it could be the way she felt when she was with him. *Free.*

It was a feeling she'd longed for, and it thrilled and scared her.

She buried her nerves in a kiss. Julia pressed her lips to his jawline, then tangled her fingers in his wet hair, the contact temporarily distracting her from what she knew was coming. The moment when she'd have to tell him something about her past.

"What about you?" he asked, and there it was. Her turn to share.

"You want to know my skeletons?" she said, slipping her hand down his chest, drawing a line across his fabulously firm body in an effort to rattle his focus. His breathing quickened, and his dick rose up in the water. But he reached for her hand before she could touch him.

"Don't distract me. We're talking," he said, in a tone that was playful but firm.

She pretended to pout. "But other things are more fun than talking."

"We'll get to other things, gorgeous. I promise you I have many things planned for you."

"But I have to 'fess up about the nudist colony I used to belong to first?"

"Yeah," he said with a grin, as he shifted her around so she lay against his body, her back to his front, his hard cock against her backside.

"And my days working in a high-class call ring with your lawyer friend?"

"Ha, that too."

"Fine," she said, ripping off the Band-Aid. "I have an ex named Donovan. We dated on and off for a few years. He was handsome and hung—"

"Hey, now."

"Well, not like you," she said, wriggling her rear against that evidence of how very well hung Clay Nichols was. So well. So unbelievably endowed in the length and width department. She thanked her lucky stars for that.

"Not like I'm even worried about that at all. I just don't want to hear about another man's prowess."

"Did I say he had prowess?"

"Julia," he said with a sigh. "Has anyone ever told you you're evasive?"

"Fine. How's this for non-evasive? Donovan and his schlong are history. But there was this other guy, Dillon. He was a photographer, and did some work shooting homes for realtors, making sure the rooms looked amazing and huge in all the pictures, and he also contracted with some companies in the city, taking product shots," she said, but didn't add the type of products he captured—like Charlie's limos. Nor did she add that while Charlie really did own and lease a fleet of limos, his limo company was pretty much his only legit operation. His other businesses were more of the racketeering variety, she suspected, and she had a hunch Charlie's Limos did some laundering too. Or so Dillon had told her. She operated on a "don't ask" policy when it came to Charlie. She didn't want to know about his business dealings; she already knew too much from the things Dillon had told her. It had all seemed playful at the time, when he'd come home from a photo shoot of a new stretch limo and flash a wad of greenbacks. "He paid me in cash again. I think Charlie's allergic to checks," he'd say.

"What a terrible affliction."

"They make him break out in hives."

"Receipts probably do too," she'd joked. Little had she known that Dillon was onto something, all right. He'd been dabbling with a most dangerous type of client.

"Anyway, we were together for a while," she said to Clay, pushing thoughts of exes far out of her mind. "But it was kind of fading out for the last several months. And well, truth be told, I honestly don't even know where he is."

"Really?"

"Yeah, really. It ended, and he's not even in San Francisco anymore," she said, and that was all true. Dillon had left. She had no clue where he'd gone. She had her suspicions. The Cayman Islands. Maybe Mexico. Someplace untraceable. Unfindable. Drinking Pina Coladas on the beach and having the last laugh. Yep. The laugh was on her. That was the other reason she kept her own secrets. She was ashamed, so terribly ashamed of how Dillon had tricked her. She'd been conned, and she didn't want anyone to know she'd been played for a fool.

"Why'd it end?"

"I told you. We drifted apart. Isn't that how it usually ends?"

"Usually."

"But Clay?"

"Yeah?"

"I don't want to talk about exes anymore. We've done that, and here I am in the bathtub with you, and candles are lit and music is playing, and you're hard because you're always hard, and it seems like now would be a good time for us to stop talking and start doing other things."

She stood up, reached for a towel, and dried off. Within a minute she was in his closet, selecting a white shirt and a cobalt blue tie to wear.

CHAPTER TEN

Lucky tie.

Knotted loosely at her neck, his power tie hung enticingly between her breasts, traveling down to her luscious belly button, then, like an arrow, pointing to the treasure that lay beneath her black lace panties.

She wore one of his shirts, freshly laundered and unbuttoned, and a pair of black stockings and heels.

Hottest. Outfit. Ever.

"Sit down, Mister," she instructed, pointing to the gray chair in the corner of his bedroom. The chair was usually home to whatever tie or shirt he'd tossed off at the end of the day. Now, he was parked in it, leaning back, getting ready for a show. He wore only a white towel, wrapped around his waist. His hair was wet from the bath.

She leaned forward, pressing play on her phone, giving him a delicious view of her breasts. Christina Aguilera's "Candyman" filled his bedroom, the pulsing beat deepening the already sexy mood. The lights were low, except for the one by the nightstand. He wasn't turning them off. He wanted to watch. He wanted to see everything.

As the opening notes sounded, she strutted over to him, and traced her fingernails along his neck, heating up his skin. "Welcome to the Girls in Ties club," she said with a purr.

"My favorite kind of club."

She ran her hand down his arm; her touch felt electric. "I have a feeling you will like our services."

"Does this club allow touching, ma'am? I don't want to break any rules."

"Only with certain patrons," she said, then swiveled around and walked in the other direction, giving him a fantastic look at her ass in her thong underwear. What he wouldn't do to tear that underwear off with his teeth right now. Bend her over, get on his knees, and pull hard till they ripped off, revealing her beautiful, wet pussy.

His imagination was already in overdrive. She turned, bent forward and shook out her gorgeous hair, and strands of sleek, wet red tumbled along her legs. When she flipped up her head, she swayed her hips back and forth.

Provocatively.

Oh so provocatively that his cock made a full tent of the towel.

She eyed his erection, her lips curving up in a wicked grin. "I see our club pleases you."

"It pleases me so very much," he said.

"Let's see if we can help you appreciate it here even more," she said, pressing her hands to her belly, then running them up her stomach.

She began to play with the buttons on his shirt, peekaboo, showing one breast, then hiding it under the fabric, then the other. She yanked the shirt closed, feigning innocence as she spun around, her hands on her knees now, shaking that delicious ass for him as the chorus of the song played loud.

A growl rose up in his chest, and his dick throbbed. He ached to take her, to touch her, to be inside her. He was a high-tension wire. Taut. But he waited patiently, his hands on his thighs, letting her play the part as she returned to him, her heels clicking against the hard wood floor.

When she reached him, she set her hands on his legs, slowly shimmying her hips as she danced. "The staff at Girls in Ties says you ordered a lap dance."

"Did I now?"

She trailed a hand along his thigh, teasing him with her nearness to his cock. "Did you want one?"

"I do when you take off that shirt."

She arched an eyebrow and opened one side of his shirt, then pressed her right breast against his chest. "Can I do this then?"

"Yes," he grunted, his entire body rigid as he refused to move, to give into his desire to touch her all over, and to be touched.

She opened the other side now, revealing her chest to him. "And this?" She moved in closer, as if she were a cat arching its back as she rubbed her breasts against him. He inhaled sharply through his nostrils. His fingers twitched with the desire to grab her hips, and slam her down on his painfully hard erection. But he kept his palms spread on his legs as she tugged off one sleeve, then another, dropping the white shirt onto the floor. She turned around, wearing only her thong, stockings, heels and his tie. She lowered herself onto his thighs, still covered in his towel.

"Oh my, it seems you like a lap dance, don't you?"

"Yes," he said in a strained voice, his hands itching to hold her.

She gyrated up and down, teasing him as she brought her delicious ass dangerously close to his erection, but not close enough. She wriggled lower, and once, just once, ground against him. He hissed out a harsh breath. He could feel her heat through his towel.

"You're soaked," he said.

She turned around, planting one high-heeled foot on the arm of the chair, the other firmly on the ground as she rocked her hips towards him. "No, sir. I am slippery. I thought we established this already."

"Let me find out how wet you are."

"Only if I can find out how hard you are," she said, punctuating her retort with a thrust of her hips close to his face. He could smell her arousal, the delicious scent of her pussy so near to him. He wanted to inhale her, to be drenched in her juices. No longer able to restrain himself, he lifted a hand, and hooked his finger into the waistband of her panties, stretching the cotton panel against her.

"Oh," she said playfully, eyeing his hand. "Are these in your way?"

"Yes. They are obstructing my view. I want to see how you look right now," he said, then slid the panties down her legs. His breathing turned erratic as he watched her be revealed, the tiniest thread of her silky desire glistening from her lips to her underwear like a trail of evidence as he pulled off the scrap of fabric. He couldn't take it anymore. He needed to taste her, to drown his mouth in her scent, to feel her wetness all over his face.

But more than that, he wanted her screams of passion to fill his ears. He wanted to see reckless desire smashing through her body. He wanted to control her pleasure. As she began to open his towel, he grabbed her hand to stop her. "No."

"I can't touch you?"

"Not yet. Go get on my bed," he said, letting her know he was taking the reins now.

"The dance is over?"

"The dance is fucking over, and I'm going to show you what you did to me," he said as he stood, tearing off the towel, letting her know how much he wanted her. Her eyes darkened with lust as she stared at his cock. Her reaction made him hotter, harder.

"I'm being punished for turning you on?"

Another shake of his head. "No. You are being rewarded for turning me on. But we're doing it my way. You teased the fuck out of me, and now I want to watch you squirm. Crawl up on my bed and get on your hands and knees."

She held up her wrists, a sexy wink in her eyes. "I've been waiting for this."

"Go, woman. And leave your shoes and stockings on."

She strutted over to the bed. He followed, watching as she climbed up, and positioned herself on all fours in the middle of the white comforter on his king-size bed. His tie dangled down from her neck onto the covers. He joined her on the bed, bending over her, and reaching his hands around to her neck. "I'm going to untie this now, and use it for something else," he said, quickly unknotting it. The tie fell into his hands as she rocked back into him. He brought a hand down to her ass, spanking her hard.

"Did I say you should rock your ass against me?"

"No."

"Do you want to be spanked again?"

"Maybe I do," she said in that taunting voice, wriggling against him once more.

She was rewarded with another smack, and that drew out a long low moan as she arched her back.

"I'll check to see how much you like it," he said, dipping his hand between her legs to test her love of spanking. Oh yeah, there was the proof, so he slapped her once more, and she drew in a sharp quick breath.

Then he tugged her hands together, sending her falling forward onto her elbows. He wrapped his tie around her wrists, once, twice, then pulled it between them to tighten the hold. Finishing it off with a strong knot, he tied the loose end to the headboard. He grabbed a pillow, and stuffed it under her chest. "This is if you need to muffle your screams."

"Assuming you make me scream," she said.

"I will make you scream, Julia. I will make sure the neighbors know how good you're about to get it."

He moved to appraise his handiwork. She was on her knees and elbows, her hands bound together with his cobalt blue tie through the slats in the headboard, her gorgeous body stretched taut.

"Mmm," he murmured, stroking his chin. "Fucking perfect."

"So now what?"

"Now, I am going to tease the ever loving fuck out of you, gorgeous," he said, and ran his hands from her shoulders down her sexy back to her ass. Placing his thumbs on that most favorite spot where her legs met her ass, he spread her cheeks. "You have the most perfect ass I have ever seen. The things I could do with this ass," he mused.

"What sort of things?"

"Oh, you'll see," he said, teasing her with his thumbs, dragging them gently between her legs. "Did dancing for me get you hot? Don't sass me, or I will take my hands off of you," he said sliding one finger lightly across her entrance.

"Yes," she whispered.

"Could you feel your panties getting hotter with each move you made on me?" He rubbed his finger lightly against her swollen clit, and she moaned, lifting her rear higher. An invitation. A beautiful fucking invitation as she showed him with her body, with her moves, how much she wanted this.

"Yes. I could feel myself getting all hot and bothered, Clay."

"Tell me what it felt like."

"I felt like I was on fire between my legs. I was aching and practically gushing in my panties," she said, her words making him groan as he pushed his thumbs against her soft flesh.

"It made me so hard to see you strutting around my house, wearing my clothes, tying my tie, and teasing the fuck out of me," he told her. "You want to see how much?"

"Yes, please."

He let go of her ass, and dragged the head of his cock against her, coating himself with her glorious wetness. A low rumbling took hold in his chest at the feel of her, so wet, so ready.

She whimpered when he pulled away.

"But I'm not giving it to you just yet." He grabbed her ass hard, spreading her legs open wider, giving him the perfect view of her glistening pussy that was so damn tempting he could not resist burying his face between her legs. The second he made contact she groaned his name, a plaintive plea for more of his tongue. But he didn't plan to give her his tongue right now, so he flicked once against her clit, then stopped.

"That is for teasing me," he said sharply.

"*Clay*," she cried.

"What do you want, gorgeous? Tell me what you want."

"I want more."

"No, you want to be fucked. I can see it as I stare at this beautiful sight," he said, returning his hand between her legs, and cupping her. "You're making my whole hand wet."

"Because I want you," she said, and he could hear the need in her voice turning into a ragged kind of desperation.

"I would be a cruel bastard to deny your pussy right now," he said, then plunged a finger inside her, and instantly, she screamed.

He thrust his finger in and out, bringing his other hand around to squeeze one of her breasts. He was bent over her, fucking her hard with a finger, and kneading her breasts, all while she could do nothing but rock into his hand.

She tightened around his finger.

"You needed more you said?" he asked.

"God, yes."

He thrust two fingers inside her, and felt her clench against him, her pussy drenching him with her arousal. "Now fuck my hand, Julia. Fuck my hand like you fuck your own fingers when you masturbate."

"You think I masturbate to you?"

"I know you do, gorgeous. I know you do. Now show me how or I'll stop," he said, pausing inside her, giving her the chance to feel what it was like to want to be fucked badly. Within seconds, she rocked into his fingers.

"That's how," she said, her breathing rushed, as she pumped herself onto his hand, thrusting up and down on his two fingers. "That's how I fucked my own fingers when I got off to you this week."

"I like it when you tell me the truth. Because when you do, I can reward you the way I like. Now, you keep riding my hand, and I want to feel you come all over me," he said, rubbing his thumb against her wet and throbbing clit as she rode him, and soon he felt her tighten all over his fingers.

She pushed back hard then screamed his name, her entire body writhing against his hand. Her noises echoed around his house, and soon, but not too soon, she slowed down. It was then that he nibbled on her bottom, and the next sound from Julia was one of surprise.

* * *

She gasped.

She was in another world right now, blissed out beyond any and all recognition. Barely aware anymore of what he was doing to her. Drugged out on his touch, her whole body felt boneless and beautiful at the same time. And he wasn't done with her. Not in the least. His hands were sliding all along her back, so firm and strong as he mapped her with his fingers, all while kissing the outline of her rear.

Her ass was in the air, and it was his for the playing. She had no clue how far he planned to go, or if she'd let him. Probably not *that* far, but she couldn't deny the way her insides melted as he ran his tongue along her ass, tracing the cheeks, then dipping down between her legs, darting against her molten center.

She could barely form words now. Could hardly talk after that orgasm. All she could manage was his name. "*Clay.*"

"I got this," he whispered. "I'll take care of you."

"I know," she murmured, sounding and feeling thoroughly intoxicated.

He returned to his kissing, this time beginning at the back of her knees, so he could lick his way up her thighs.

"Oh God," she whimpered, because his tongue was magic. He returned to her backside, flicking his tongue across her flesh, and then he kissed her between her legs. She wasn't sure if her pussy could handle it right now, being worked over by his epic mouth, but she was willing to see. But then, maybe that's not where he was headed.

Because . . . oh . . .

Was his tongue *there*? Was it supposed to feel that good? Her body answered for her, and she rocked back into him. A long needy moan escaped her throat as he flicked his tongue against her ass, spreading her cheeks wider with his thumbs. She felt so vulnerable, so open to him right now, and though some part of her was tempted to toss out a snarky comment, she was without words as he licked her, surprising her with how very much she enjoyed where his tongue was. Only him, only this man could get away with doing that. Tenderly, he pressed his thumbs against her cheeks, rubbing a finger along her pussy gently, all while licking her ass.

Sensations flooded her veins, pleasure pulsing through her body as he touched her in new ways, showing her what a masterful lover he was and how much he delighted in pleasing her. Because he did please. Oh, did he ever. Hot flames spread inside her, lighting up her skin as he worked his tongue against her rear with quick, hard flicks.

Soon, she felt her belly tighten, her sex clench, and she called out his name as another orgasm roared through her, chasing waves of pleasure all the way to her fingertips. Her vision blurred as she squeezed her eyes shut, giving in to the sensations, to the way he simply took her and led her down this path of absolute and pure pleasure. She sank down onto her elbows, her back bowing. She was damn near about to collapse, but she still wanted more of him.

"Keep that ass up in the air, gorgeous," he said, and she heard him tearing open a condom wrapper and rolling one on. He smoothed his hands along the backs of her thighs, causing her to quiver, as he lifted her ass higher, giving him the access he wanted to her pussy.

In one quick move, he was inside her, his hard length filling her so completely that she was sure this was the definition of intensity. She moaned and rasped out his name. "Clay. It feels so good to have you inside me."

"There's no place else I want to be right now," he said, wrapping his hands around her hips, holding her tight. "Look at you," he said, as he thrust into her, his cock stretching her so exquisitely that it was almost unfair to feel this good. "On your hands and knees, all tied up on my bed. Your perfect fucking body, here for me to take."

"You can take me anyway you want," she said, her voice more hot and bothered than it had ever been.

"I want to take you in every way possible," he said, driving deeper into her, his cock scraping across her swollen clit with each delirious thrust. "Watch you writhe in pleasure. Knowing I did that to you."

She wriggled against him, showing him how she moved for him. "Like this? You like when you make me writhe like this?"

"Yeah, it makes me harder," he said, his voice turning hoarse as he started to pump faster.

She could barely move with her hands tied to the headboard, but she didn't need to, because he was making sure she was in heaven again, taking her, sliding into her, gripping her hips the whole time. She rocked back into him, picking up the rhythm too, and soon they were in an achingly sinful synch.

"You're going to come again," he said roughly, bending over her back, his chest touching her as he braced himself with his hands on the bed. He covered her completely, and there was little she could do, but little she needed because this was all instinct, all natural, all intense pleasure that tore through her body. He gripped her tied-up wrists, holding them tight as he thrust deeper into her, taking her like he owned her.

Tonight he did. And though she hating being owned, in this moment she relished it. She savored it, thrilling at the feel of this strong man controlling every ounce of her pleasure and every square inch of her body. She was barely aware of how loud she was, of the sounds that escaped her lips, the animal-like cries as he filled her to the hilt.

But soon, she was heading for the cliff and he was riding her there, charging headfirst into another climax. "Bite down on the pillow when I make you come again," he said.

She muffled her screams as she raced to the other side, shattering into pure white-hot bliss.

"You make me come so fucking hard, Julia. So. Fucking. Hard," he said, driving into her, as he joined her.

CHAPTER ELEVEN

The moon glowed overhead, bathing the balcony in a shimmery light. Julia was snuggled in one of Clay's sweatshirts. It had the name of his alma mater across the front, and for some reason that made her like wearing it even more. Maybe because it was not only his, but it also said something about him. He was a man who knew his stuff. He was passionate about his work, dedicated, driven.

But then, Dillon had known his stuff too, hadn't he? He was a passionate photographer, until, well, until he took off. Hell, maybe he was shooting beach shots somewhere. She hadn't a clue.

She angled her chopsticks into the carton of pad thai, dug out some noodles and took a bite. Lounging across an outdoor bench, her legs rested on his thighs. He'd covered the bench with a blanket because the wood was damp from the earlier rain. Now, the night sky was quiet, and the faint hints of the earlier storm clung to the air.

He was clad in boxer briefs and a T-shirt that showed off his sexy, sculpted arms. She found herself enjoying the view immensely, even though she'd enjoyed plenty of views of him undressed already. He was ogle-able at all times—in a dress shirt, in a T-shirt, in his birthday suit.

"Mmm. This hits the spot."

He took a bite of the noodles too. "We worked up an appetite."

"I'll say," she said, then set the carton down on the table. He reached for her legs and began rubbing her calves, gently massaging them with his strong hands.

She stretched and wiggled closer, delighting in the relaxing feel of his firm hands sending a new kind of pleasure through her, one that made her muscles sing, and her veins flood with warmth. "You are too good to me," she murmured.

"Only way I want to be," he said and sighed happily, a contented sound as he rubbed her legs, then moved down to her feet, cupping her ankle in one hand as he massaged the arch of her foot with his thumbs. "I figure your feet can use this, with those crazy heels you wear."

"I like my crazy heels."

"I love your crazy heels, and I want to make sure you can keep wearing them."

"How do you like them best?" she said, playfully.

"With your legs wrapped around my neck."

She smiled at him, a woozy sort of contentment bathing the night. "What time is it? I feel like I lost all sense of the world around me tonight."

He bent down to kiss her shin. "Good. That's how it should be. And to answer your question, it's nearly midnight."

A brief hit of tension touched down in her body, like an alarm. Tomorrow night at this time, she'd be headed home. This weekend—perfect as it was—would be over. It would be a delicious memory, but only that. A slice of her life that was in the past.

There was a part of her that wanted to stop time, and live in this escape to New York for a while, forget her debts, forget her obligations, forget Kim and her hubby and the rest of the employees at Cubic Z. Ignore the whole wide world and live in this bubble of sex and chemistry and the delicious sort of getting-to-know-you that fools a person into falling. Boy, was she falling for him, headfirst into a crazy kind of like, the kind that made her want to send him sweet texts and naughty texts, that made her want to talk to him about everything and nothing, that made her want to hear all about his day. Every day.

To be the first person he saw in the morning, and the last one he saw at night.

What a crazy notion. She must he high. Intoxicated on epic sex. She needed to clear her orgasm-clouded head.

"So, Miss Julia. How's this going to work out?"

She raised an eyebrow inquisitively. "What do you mean?"

He pointed from her to him, speaking in a clear, firm voice. "You and me. I don't want this to just be a one-time thing. I want to see you again."

She fixed him with a quizzical look. Surely, he wasn't the kind of man who wanted a long-distance relationship. But then, he said he'd been with Sabrina for a while, and she had no reason to believe he was a player, or a ladies man either. And while she wasn't sure what she wanted from him, she did know one thing for certain: she wanted to see him again. He'd rocked her world in more ways than one. With pleasure, and with laughs, and with the tender ways he had. That was the problem—he was so good for her, and she simply had no real estate in her life for this kind of potential. One of them or both of them would wind up hurt.

But she had enough problems, so she made a split-second choice—to be abundantly honest in this instant about how she felt. "I would like that," she said, without agenda, without teasing. "I live on the other side of the country though."

"I am aware of that, and I want to see you again and again. You're not seeing anyone else, are you?"

She rolled her eyes. "No, of course not. I wouldn't do that."

"And you like being with me presumably?"

"Obviously."

"So let's do this," he said in the most matter-of-fact tone. As if a relationship spanning three thousand miles were truly that easy.

"How? How are we supposed to pull this off?" As much as she liked him, long-distance love affairs had a gigantic built-in roadblock.

"There's this thing called an airplane," he said dryly. "It flies. You get on it. I get on it. We both get off on the other side."

"Oh ha ha, funny guy."

"Why thank you very much. I like to make sure all departments are fully functional, including the humor one."

"Well, it is. But I do work a ton, you know," she said, her natural instinct to erect walls rearing its head.

"As do I."

"So it might not be that often that we can see each other."

"If you are not interested in this continuing, you should just say so, rather than point out the obstacles," he said, his dark eyes fixed on hers, his gaze serious and intense.

She opened her mouth to speak, but it was as if she'd been injected with an overdose of nerves. One she needed to ignore. "I am interested in this continuing," she said, and it felt like an admission, as if she were confessing something hard but true. Because this was only supposed to be one weekend. This wasn't supposed to be more. But the idea of this— them—ending after one weekend felt like a stone in her chest.

"Good," he said, running his fingers across her calf. His touch was something she was already used to, and already going to miss desperately. "We will manage what we can then."

"Okay, but it might get expensive."

"I don't know how to break this to you gently, so I'm just going to be blunt. I do well for myself. I have frequent flyer miles and a credit card that works."

She heaved out a playful sigh, even though inside that was part of what worried her, and a big part of why she needed to keep him not just at an arm's length, but a football-field length from Charlie. He'd find a way to blackmail him, tie him up into all sorts of trouble. A prominent lawyer boasting a client list teeming with money? He'd have a field day with Clay.

"I want to see you, and I will buy you tickets and buy my own," he continued. "I also have clients in San Francisco, and Los Angeles, and I get to the west coast a lot."

"I am sure, but I don't want you paying for me. I don't like owing people," she said with firmness to her tone. She didn't want to be in anyone's debt ever again.

"I don't want to be paid back. I want to see you. I'm not buying you. I'm saying I want to date you, and some dates require a cab, and some require a town car, and some require an airline ticket. And if that's the cost of transportation—an airline ticket—if that's my fare from New York to San Fran, I don't see how that's any different than if you lived in Brooklyn and came to see me here in Manhattan over the weekend," he said, keeping his eyes locked on her the whole time as he spoke with such confidence.

"I guess, but I don't want to feel like I'm a kept woman," she said, even though she relished the idea of seeing him. He'd made a more-than-convincing argument that they should make a go of things.

He laughed hard. "No one ever in the whole wide world could keep you. I'm just going to be happy if I can spend a few hours with you."

"You like the sex that much?" she said, playfully pushing her toes against his hard abs.

"You know I like the sex. I think the part that's not getting through to you is how very much I like all the other parts. I like what's in here," he said, stretching across her to tap her forehead with his index finger, "And I like doing the things here," he said, sweeping his thumb across her lips, "that involve talking." He traveled down her chest, tracing a line between her breasts, and landing on her heart. "I also like the things I'm seeing in here."

Her heart beat in double time, and it was such a foreign feeling for her; it had been so long since she'd *felt* for someone. It scared her, but felt wonderful at the same time, too. But then, wasn't that what liking someone felt like? A little bit like stepping off the diving board, and taking the plunge? She grasped his hand, clutched it in hers, holding his against her chest. His eyes sparkled with happiness, a genuine sort of joy, as if she'd just said yes to him. Which, she supposed, she had.

"So you're gonna be my boyfriend?"

"Gorgeous, I'm not your boyfriend. I'm your lover. The only one."

"Obviously. You are my only lover. No woman could ever have you and want or need another man."

"Good. Now remember what I was saying about liking all the things we do?"

She nodded. "Yeah?"

He leaned across the bench, kissed her lips gently, then brushed them with his fingertips. The slightest kiss sent tingles through her. "I could do that and other things all night. But right now, I want you to use those lips to tell me more about you. You said your best friend is your sister. Besides your hair stylist, Gayle. Were you close to McKenna growing up, or did you become best friends later?"

Her eyes widened. She was impressed that he remembered all the details, down to her hairdresser's name. "We've always been close. We're one year apart. Irish twins, as they say. We fought like sisters do, but most of the time, we were like this," she said, twisting her index finger around her middle finger.

"Read the same books, liked the same TV shows. We were both huge *My So-Called Life* junkies. The show was only on for one season, but we watched all the episodes over and over on cable, and recited the lines together, and we loved Jordan Catalano too from that show. So McKenna and I had this thing in high school when we started dating that we'd always check in on the other with a phone call."

"Ah, the old 'friend emergency call,' he said, sketching air quotes.

"Yup," she said, nodding proudly. "But our deal was if one of us was having a bad time and needed to be saved, that person would say *I can't believe Jordan's arm is broken.* And if we were having a good time and really liked a guy we'd say, *You're watching My So-Called Life* right now?"

"Ring, ring. McKenna's calling. You better pick up."

Julia mimed answering a phone. "Hey McKenna, how's it going?" she said into her pretend phone. She paused as if listening. "Oh, I'm so glad Jordan's arm isn't broken." She locked eyes with Clay, and he grinned as she continued her phone call. "What did you say? You're watching *My So-Called Life* right now?" His smile widened, lighting up his whole gorgeous face. "That is the best show. Well, you have a good time, because I am having the best time."

She hung up her imaginary phone and ran her fingers across his stubbled jaw, rough with his more than five-o'clock shadow. "You, Mister, are better than *My*

So-Called Life," she said, and was surprised by how easily the admission rolled off her tongue. This was precisely what she hadn't wanted to happen this weekend. *To feel.* To want. To have strings start to attach themselves that would extend well beyond a weekend.

But here she was, making plans, making commitments, telling him exactly how she felt.

What was she getting herself into? She needed to put on the brakes and deal with her debt first. But then Clay's mouth was on her, kissing her hard and hungry again, consuming her with his lips that made her bones vibrate and her blood sing, and all thoughts of brakes and debts and troubles turned to rubble in her brain, because desire had slammed hard into her body.

He picked her up in his arms, carried her inside, up the steps and into his bed. This time there were no ties, no binds, no hard, rough hands, though she had loved all of that.

Now, he simply laid her on his bed and kissed her from head to toe, his lips melting her from the inside out. She trembled, both from the way he touched her and from her heart thundering with hope for what they could be. They could be so good for each other. He entered her, taking his time, making slow, sweet, luxurious love to her as she wrapped her arms and her legs around him, reveling in all the ways they came together.

CHAPTER TWELVE

Brunch sounded nice. Julia envisioned one of those lazy New York mornings. They'd make love, then shower, then wander around the Village, stumble into some fantastic four-table restaurant that had fabulous French toast or decadent omelets. Wait, no. She had a better idea. They'd go to a diner, because diners in New York were the best ever, and diners in San Francisco could suck it. At the booth, his hands would be all over her, touching her back, her waist, her legs. They'd return to his place, unable to stop touching, then smash into each other in the elevator and fall into his apartment already in a state of undress. Fevered and frenzied, he'd take her one last time, the kind of urgent and desperate goodbye sex that would make them both miss each other terribly when she left for the airport an hour later, waving goodbye in her taxi, trying hard not to stare out the window the entire time as the cab drove away.

She stretched her arms over her head, enjoying that fantasy as morning sun streaked in the window, painting the bedroom in the early glow of dawn. Clay was a sound sleeper, and lay snoozing on his stomach, the covers hitting his hips. His gorgeous back, strong and muscled, was on display. She was tempted to reach out and touch him, trace lazy lines down his skin, but a light flashed on the nightstand.

Grabbing her phone, she headed into the bathroom and scrolled through her messages as she brushed her teeth.

First there was Kim saying they'd had a rocking Saturday night and raked in some serious money. Next, McKenna, saying Chris's TV show had hit an all-time high in ratings, and the network execs were talking to him about renewals. The note was followed by several exclamation points.

Then there was a message from Charlie.

Julia tensed as she opened it.

We have a big whale in town tonight. We're moving up the game. Need to see you there by nine. There is a chance for you to get a lot closer if you can take him down.

She wrote back quickly. *Can't. I won't be back till eleven.*

She set the phone down on the sink counter, finished brushing her teeth, and rinsed with a glass of water. Her phone buzzed again. *Perhaps you mistook that for a request. It was not. I will see you at nine.*

Anger slithered through her, hot, black anger at Charlie, at Dillon, at all the ways she was indebted to those two. She clicked on the message and dialed Charlie's number.

He answered on the second ring.

"I am not in town," she whispered through gritted teeth. "I can't be there."

"Red, I have seen the airline schedules. I even checked for you. And there will be a ticket waiting for you on the eleven a.m. flight back. It gets you into town at two-thirty, so you will have plenty of time to make yourself beautiful and show off those lovely breasts to help distract our high roller."

She squeezed her eyes shut, clenched her free hand, feeling like his prostitute. Like his dirty little trick to lure them in, because that's what she was. A woman used.

"Don't you get it?" she said in a low voice, not wanting Clay to hear, though the bathroom door was closed. "I can't."

"But you can. And you will. And if you don't, I will be happy to visit your bar more frequently. After all, it may very well be my bar someday soon. How do you think your pretty little friend with the baby in her belly would like working with me? Maybe we can even put her little one to work for me soon too," he said, and her insides churned with the thought. Images of sweet Kim and her family becoming part of Charlie's circle of indentured servitude made her want to vomit. Not to mention hang her head further in shame. "But I haven't decided if I will keep Cubic Z open, or if I will take great pleasure in driving it into the ground, and all that money you needed for your bar will be for naught. But you will have the reminder in front of your face to never try to take my money again," he said, and it was as if his foot were on her chest, digging in, keeping her pinned and prostrate under all his weight. "Unless you come back, and you play and you win."

If there was one thing Julia had learned in this lifetime, and in these few months being on Charlie's very short leash, it was that whoever had the leverage won. There was no bluffing when you owed money to someone who lived on his own side of the law, who operated by his rules. Call him a mobster, call him a gangster, she didn't care about the semantics. A real Tony Soprano but without the Italian heritage, Charlie was like Tony in the sense that he was the man, he was in charge, and you didn't fuck with him. There was no need for a poker face for Charlie because her cards were shit. He had a royal flush. He could take what he wanted from her. She knew of his ways, had heard of all the things he'd done, how he made sure money and debts were always paid to him, and for much more than the debtor bargained for.

The interest he charged damn near killed you.

When you owed him, he owned you and that meant everyone you cared about was in line if you couldn't pay the vig. Soon, he'd encroach further, plucking at her family, her friends, all her loved ones. She couldn't take the risk of pissing him off. He'd hurt someone to punish her for her impudence. She had no choice but to abide by his wishes.

"Fine. I will see you tonight."

She stabbed the end button on her screen, but it was thoroughly unsatisfying. She pushed both hands roughly through her hair, grabbing hard against her scalp, something, *anything* to unleash her agitation. She wanted to shake a fist at the sky, to slam her phone onto the floor. But in the end, she'd have to do what Charlie told her to do. Come home, slide into a tight black dress, and too-high heels, and sit down at the table ready to be ogled and to win. She was his secret weapon, a one-two punch with boobs and talent.

She looked at the time. The flight he wanted her on left in two hours.

The back of her eyes burned, the start of a thick sob threatening her. She inhaled sharply, drawing her hurt back inside, sucking it down. She was a fool for thinking she could manage any sort of relationship while she was still clawing her way out of the mess her last relationship had left for her. But that's what she was— a fool, a mark, a pawn. She'd been taken, Dillon had scammed her, and she had no clue it was happening until it was done. Damn him, leaving her saddled with this while he got off scot-free. Leaving her no choice but to walk away from a man she was starting to feel real things for.

But feeling more for Clay would only put him in the line of fire. She had to extricate herself before she made her problems his problems. No one wanted that kind of shit in their lives.

* * *

She was stuffing her clothes in her suitcase. Clay rubbed his eyes, and covered his mouth as he yawned. Maybe he was seeing things, but it sure looked like Julia was fixing to get the hell out of Dodge. Dressed in jeans and a sweater, she was tugging the zipper closed on her suitcase.

"I thought your flight wasn't till five," he said, scrubbing his hand across his jaw.

She shook her head. "I got it wrong. I transposed the times. It's 11:05, not 5:11."

"Let's just change it then."

"I tried. The later flight is booked," she said, and her voice was strained, as if she were speaking through a sieve.

"Really?" He arched an eyebrow.

"Yes, really," she said, but she didn't look at him. She kept tugging and yanking at her suitcase. He got out of bed to help, kneeling down on the floor next to her. His shoulder bumped hers, and she cringed as if he'd burned her.

"You okay?"

"Yeah, fine," she said, crisply as he closed the suitcase for her.

"You don't seem fine."

"I just need to go, that's all. I hate being late and missing flights. It totally stresses me out," she said, and there was a hitch in her voice, as if she were about to cry. Did she have some kind of bad childhood memory about missing a flight? Because she sure as hell seemed sadder than the moment warranted.

"Let me go with you then to the airport. We can at least spend more time together in the car."

She shook her head. "That's sweet. But I just have to go. The cab is already here." She stood up. "I need to get going. I'm going to have to work tonight, too."

He cocked his head to the side, saying nothing, just studying her. He was used to negotiations, to deal-making, to knowing when someone was lying, and his hackles were raised.

She didn't seem so stressed or sad anymore. She seemed full of shit.

"Which one is it, Julia?" His words came out more harshly than he'd thought. Or maybe they were exactly as harsh as he felt. "Are you working tonight or did you mix up your flights? Because I'd buy one, or maybe I'd buy the other, but two seems like you're piling on the excuses."

She huffed out through her nostrils, narrowed her eyes. "Do not even think about accusing me of lying."

"I did not accuse. I asked," he said. "But it's interesting to see where your brain went."

Her eyes widened, and they were filled with anger. "I have to go," she said, biting out the words. "I need to get out of here. I have shit to take care of at home, and that is that. I will call you later."

"I'm so sorry to hear Jordan's arm is broken," he said, not bothering to strip the anger from his voice.

She shot him a furious look, but kept her mouth shut as she grabbed her bag, headed down the steps to the front door and out of his building.

The door clanged shut, the sound of it echoing throughout his home, leaving him with cold, empty silence.

He could have gone after her. Followed her, gently grabbed her arm, and asked if she was okay, if he'd done something wrong. But there was no point. She didn't want to be stopped. She didn't need to be stopped. She was a woman who'd made up her mind, and he had enough self-pride and smarts to know he'd been played. Especially when he grabbed his computer and sank down on the couch in his living room to look up the email from Virgin Atlantic, since he'd been the one to buy the ticket for her.

His heart dropped. Hot shame spread in his chest. He had no clue what had gone wrong, but the time on the ticket told him that all this falling had been a one-way street.

She was still on the 5:11 flight.

He cursed more times than he could count as he slammed his laptop closed. He ran a hand through his hair, anger and frustration coursing through his bloodstream. The last thing he wanted to do was sit with this feeling. He pulled on workout clothes and went to the boxing gym to spend the morning punching the bag alone, letting all his anger pour out of him, and his hurt too. The stupid hurt he felt for having been left.

He'd only known her for a short time. Had only spent a few days with her. They had been perfect, fabulous wonderful days, but even so his heart shouldn't ache without her. Like a gaping hole in his chest.

It should feel like nothing.

Like nothing. He let those words echo in his head with each punishing jab until eventually his mind was blank, and his body was tired, and he hoped against hope he'd forget her fast.

CHAPTER THIRTEEN

Even-steven.

For a card player there were worse words. Like *lost it all*, or *lost big*.

But for now, the words *even-steven* stung.

That's where she'd netted out. With nothing to show for her race home to play Charlie's whale.

"You disappointed me tonight, Red. I expected more from you," he said, as he bent over a steaming bowl of noodles. He slurped up a spoonful, the noodles trailing wetly down his chin, the last one snaking into his mouth.

He pushed his index finger down hard on the ledger next to him. "This? This blank line for you tonight? This tells me you have something else on your mind. Do you?"

She shook her head, pressed her lips together as if she could hold in all the nasty things she wanted to say to him. Her fists were clenched at her sides. "No," she muttered.

He pushed back his chair, the sound of the legs scraping across the floor of the Chinese restaurant. He rose and reached for her chin, grabbing her roughly. His calloused fingers dug into her jaw so hard that he was practically pushing the inside of her cheek into her teeth. All her instincts told her to cry out, to yelp from the sharp, cruel pain. But he'd see that as a sign of weakness, and weakness had no place in his poker circuit. If she let on, he'd throw her out and find some other way to extort her. A worse way, surely.

He angled her chin, forcing her to look at him. "You lie to me, Red. You lie like you lie at the table with your poker face. You went away for the weekend to see a man, didn't you? And you can't stop thinking about him."

She rolled her eyes as if that notion were ludicrous. "I only wish I had done something so interesting. Told you I was seeing friends in New York. That's all."

"Your friends have distracted you then," he said, enunciating each word so crisply that a bead of spit flew out of his lips and landed on her skin. "Do I need to pay them a visit? Enlist them in my employ?"

"No," she shouted, as he poked at her deepest fears. "But maybe you shouldn't have called me back then. I barely got off my flight before I had to show up."

He sneered at her, his fingers drilling her face. "You had three hours in between. That is enough."

"Well, it wasn't enough tonight."

He yanked her closer to him, so close her eyes could no longer focus on his face. She stood her ground though, her high-heeled feet digging into the floor as his brutal fingers jammed her jaw. "I can't have my ringer bringing me nothing."

"Sometime you win, sometime you lose, sometimes it rains. That's the way it goes," she said in as flat a voice as she could muster.

He dropped his hold on her chin, then stared at her curiously, as if she were a science project. "I do not like baseball. Do not give me baseball analogies. Give me your best poker face and beat my whales. That is all I want from you."

"That's what you'll keep getting."

"But Red, I did not like your performance tonight. If it happens again, I will be adding on to your totals."

Her heart plunged and she wanted to shriek *no*. A loud, echoing cry that would carry through the night. "It's not even my fault. It's not even my money," she said, insistently, as if that might change his mind.

"It is your fault. It is your money. And you are mine until I say you're not," he said, rooting around in his pocket. He took out his knife, opened it, and stabbed it into the table. She cringed, and there was no hiding her emotions this time as the sound of metal parking itself into wood rattled in her ears. He didn't remove the blade; he left it standing there like some strange trophy. "Or do you want me to visit your pretty bartender friend?" he asked, making a circle over his stomach as a reminder that he knew Kim was pregnant.

Her heart twisted. "No."

"How about your sister? She's a lovely lady, and quite perky on that little fashion blog of hers," Charlie said in his cool even voice.

It was as if he'd sliced her open with his knife, her bleeding organs on display for all to see. Julia bit her lip hard, trying to stop her insides from quivering. Charlie had never gone near her family, or her friends. He'd never mentioned McKenna until now, and her heart raced at the pace of fear. She'd do anything to keep her sister away from him. "Please leave them out of this. This has nothing to do with them."

"That's right," he said with a firm nod, pointing from her to him. "It is our business, and we will continue to do business until it is all resolved, or else I might need to collect from them too. Is that clear?"

With his words, the floor felt out from under her. He'd done it. He'd done the thing she feared. Threatened her family. Fear coursed through her body, rooting itself in her belly in a twisted knot where it planned to set up camp for a long, long time. "Yes," she choked out.

"Now get out of here, and I will call you when I have a game you won't mess up."

She turned on her heels and left the restaurant, Skunk holding open the door. He lowered his voice to a whisper, as if he didn't want Charlie to hear him. "Want me to call you a cab?" he asked, and he sounded like a sweet, sympathetic bear. Like he legitimately wanted to do something nice after the way Charlie had spoken. He had some kind of soft spot for her. But she wasn't going to be fooled. She knew where his loyalties lay and it wasn't with the woman he wanted to help. It was with the man who owned him, just as Charlie owned nearly everyone he worked with.

Except her. She told herself Charlie only rented her, and eventually the lease would be up.

"No thank you. I don't need a cab," she said, and walked home, the fog crawling into the city, threatening to ensnare the night. She brushed her hand roughly against her cheek, wiping away a tear.

But another one fell, and then another, and that's how she walked home, wishing there were a way to unravel herself faster from Charlie's clutches. Wishing she'd never met Dillon, that he'd never made off with $100,000 from the mobster he worked for, and that he'd never claimed the money was for her.

When she reached her home and poured herself a glass of whiskey, her fingers itched to pick up the phone and call Clay. To tell him why she ran, that she missed him, and that this weekend was the best she'd ever had.

But she could still feel Charlie's hand on her chin, and she knew, she fucking knew she shouldn't be involved with anyone. Because when you get close to people, your debt becomes their debt, and theirs becomes yours, and you are left with nothing but an aching well of shame inside you as you try to claw your way out.

Clay could be just like Dillon—disappearing, and leaving her holding all his problems.

She put the phone in a kitchen drawer and shut it hard.

* * *

"Uncross your legs," Gayle said, pointing her sharp scissors at Julia.

"You have the weapon. I do as you say," Julia said, following orders. "But why is it that I see you every six weeks and I still can't remember to uncross my legs when you start trimming?"

"Maybe because you have too much else on your mind," Gayle said, patting Julia's shoulder then widening her stance so she could trim the ends of her hair.

The stylist dressed in black as she always did, and today's homage to the shade of midnight was a black tunic top and tight leggings, with black cowboy boots on her feet. Down her arm was her permanent mark— a tattoo in a swirling script that said *I want to be adored.* Julia loved the boldness in branding her own body with a wish for love. She longed for that sort of daring. The wish had come true; Gayle had worked in New York a few times a year, cutting celebrities' hair, and on a recent trip she'd met someone recently who she'd fallen hard and fast for, and he for her. There were no issues, no problems, no pasts in the way. He'd moved here to be with her.

Of course, you never knew what was coming. When someone would turn on you. She would never have predicted Dillon would be a world-class douche. A knot of anger was set loose in her body at the thought of her ex; like a marble in a Rube Goldberg machine, it rolled down the tracks, picking up speed. Her insides were twisted, and Dillon wasn't the sole cause. She'd been wracked with tension since she left Clay behind in a swirl of dust in New York. Every night she'd been tempted to text, to call, to chat. Every night she'd resisted.

Her chest felt like a pressure valve inside her. The valve was stuck, so the pressure kept building. She tapped her toe on the hardwood floor of the salon as Gayle cut.

"What's the story, Jules? You're jumpy today."

She sighed heavily, as if the weight of the last week were pouring out in that one breath. "Oh Gayle, it's getting harder," she said, because she couldn't take it anymore. Her stylist was the only person who had a clue about the troubles Dillon had dumped on her doorstep when he'd skipped town with Charlie's money, claiming Julia would be paying it off. Julia reckoned a stylist was akin to a shrink. Maybe even a priest. A stylist was the one person you could pour out all your secrets to. Gayle wasn't a part of her regular life—she was someone she saw every six weeks. Neat and cordoned off, safe from the harm that was circling her on the other side. "I still owe a crap ton of money, and the people I owe it to aren't making it any easier for me, and on top of that, I met someone I really like, but I can't let myself get close to him because of all this stuff going on. I want to trust him, but he might screw me over too, but I miss him like crazy, which makes no sense because it was only one weekend. Okay, it was two weekends, but still, they were both spectacular," she said, the words spilling out of her. Julia stopped talking for a second, stared in the mirror at her friend's reflection. "Wow. That was like a confessional or something."

Gayle squeezed Julia's shoulder, and then continued snipping. "I'm so glad you met someone you like. It's been so long since Dillon, and even then you weren't terribly fond of the douche. With good reason, of course," she quickly added, with a wry smile.

Julia narrowed her eyes. "He is such a douche. And I feel so stupid for ever trusting him, or even getting involved with him."

"That's the thing. Sometimes you just can't know how someone is going to turn out," Gayle said as she ran a comb through Julia's wet hair, appraising her work so far.

"Right? So I guess it's all for the best that things aren't happening with this other guy. He might turn out to be just like Dillon. I was an idiot for getting involved with him, and an even worse idiot for the way he scammed me."

"That's not what I meant. I mean, you can't beat yourself up for not knowing Dillon was going to con money out of his employer and pin the debt on you," she said, because that's the extent of what she knew. Not that Charlie was a gangster, but that Dillon had swindled money from him. "That man should have his balls chopped off."

"If I ever see him again, can I borrow those scissors?"

"I'll order a better pair. A ball-snipping pair. But let's talk about happier fates for balls. What's this other guy like?" Gayle said, stopping her cutting for a moment to bump her hip against Julia's shoulder, giving her a salacious wink in the mirror. "I want to hear all about him."

She couldn't help but grin at the memories that came racing back—images that warmed her heart, and sent her body soaring. Clay's strong hands holding her down. His tongue working her over. His mouth claiming hers. Okay, now she was doing more than grinning. She was tingling something fierce. A sharp bolt of lust shot straight to her core, and then a burst of warmth surrounded her heart as she flashed on all the sweet things he'd said to her. "He's the sexiest, dirtiest, smartest, and kindest man I have ever met."

Gayle's eyes widened. "More, more. Tell me more."

She told her about their weekend. Not every detail, but enough to make Gayle's jaw drop, and the tension to loosen momentarily in Julia. Just talking about him felt good. It was as close as she was going to come to being near him, because once she left this salon she was going back on lockdown. She'd tie her hands behind her back if that was what she had to do to resist him.

CHAPTER FOURTEEN

His junior partner's jaw dropped when he saw the gift. A new set of five-irons that Flynn had been eyeing for a few weeks. Talking about. Showing him pictures of on the Internet. It had damn near gotten to the point of golf porn. But Flynn had sealed the deal with the Pinkertons yesterday, and with the kind of dough the film producers were raking in, he was contributing quite nicely to the firm's bottom line. That kind of dedication and drive needed to be rewarded.

"Holy crap," he said as he reached for the set and removed one club, touching it as if it were some kind of rare treasure. He stroked it with his palm.

"Flynn, man. You can't start feeling up the golf clubs in my office. If you do I'm going to need to take them back," Clay joked.

"I can't help myself," he said, his eyes wide as he gazed at the club in his hand. "This is a thing of beauty. Almost better than a woman."

"You haven't met the right woman then," he said, and his mind latched onto Julia, and how she'd seemed like the perfect woman for him. Smart, sharp, witty, and with that vulnerable side underneath. His mind flooded with images of their weekend: her curled up on his bench on the balcony, him washing her legs in the tub, that kiss in the rain that she'd in-sisted on. Then, to all the things they'd shared, her stories of her sister, his tales about Thanksgiving, and the easy way they had together. Like two people who were meant to be matched. Until she walked out on a lie. His chest knotted up, and his shoulders tensed, both with anger and annoyance.

Damn.

This wouldn't do. He didn't have the real estate in his head or his heart to keep going back to her, and all the ways he'd wanted her. Good thing he was seeing Michele tonight. She had a way of keeping him fo-cused on the present, not the past. "I'm out of here. Meeting a friend for drinks," he said to Flynn, then grabbed his suit jacket and took off, making some phone calls when he hit the streets of New York.

First, he rang his buddy, Cam, about their poker game this week, and to check in on some information he'd asked him to run down on another potential client—a TV producer who'd seemed a little shady when he came to him, claiming his studio had screwed him over.

"I looked into your guy, and I can see how he might seem like a crooked bastard with the way things ended with his last deal. But you know what? I checked him out six ways to Sunday and that fucker is squeaky clean as can be," Cam told him.

"Good to know," he said, relieved his gut had been wrong. It was rare when it happened, but that's why he liked to do his homework and research clients in advance.

"That's why you like me though. C'mon, admit it. You love me because you never know if someone is a slimeball, but I can *always* find out."

"That you can. And I guess I love you, in some pathetic needy way that makes me sick," he teased.

"Aww, you're so sweet when you shower me with compliments. So you gonna take this deal?"

"I probably will."

"Then cigars are on you this week. I want the finest Cubans you can get your grimy paws on, because I plan on winning all the money in your pocket," Cam said, and Clay couldn't help but laugh at his friend's brashness.

"We'll see about that," he said, and hung up to call Davis.

As it rang drops of rain began to fall. With his phone pressed to his ear, he navigated the rush hour crowds on Lexington Avenue. Women in skirts and heels and men in suits began to pop open umbrellas.

The rain wasn't hard enough or heavy enough for him to worry about getting wet though. "Are they taking care of you across the pond?" he said into the phone.

"Of course. You know the producers love me," Davis said.

"Modest as always."

"Just like you," he fired back.

"No troubles then? Anything I need to take care of?"

"You already got me that one-day-off-a-week clause so I could fly home and see Jill, so I'm doing just fine."

"Ah, I guess that's why I didn't see you when you were in New York last weekend," Clay joked, as he stopped at a red light.

"Amazing, isn't it, how I'd rather spend time with her than you?"

"Shocking," he said in a dry voice.

"What's the latest with you? What happened with the woman you were hung up on?"

Clay clenched his jaw at the mention, frustration eating away at him. He didn't feel like talking about Julia or how she'd taken off. It had been more than a week now without a word from her. He hadn't reached out to her, and he was doing his damnedest not to think about her, burying himself in work, in contracts, in doing whatever he could for his clients. That was his focus. Head down in business, and no place else. He could not tolerate a repeat of the Year of Sabrina, especially now that Flynn had reeled in the Pinkertons. He still felt guilty for losing Flynn's big action-film director client that year when his focus had been tangled up in Sabrina's troubles. Clay needed to train his associate right, and show him how to keep winning and closing deals. The Pinkertons were a prize, and he'd make sure they were treated right by his firm and given ample attention.

"She was a piece of work," he said vaguely as the light changed and he crossed, nearing the restaurant where he was meeting Michele. "I'm about to have a drink with your sister, though."

"Well, be sure to keep your damn hands off of her," Davis said in a light-hearted tone.

Clay shook his head and rolled his eyes. "Fuck off to you, too. I'll catch you later."

After hanging up, he pushed open the door, brushed off the drops of water on his suit jacket, and weaved his way to Michele, who was perched on a stool at the bar. She waved when she saw him, and as he reached her she wrapped him in a hug, and gave him a kiss on the cheek.

"You don't have an umbrella," she said, wagging her finger.

He loosened his dark-green tie, unknotting the damn thing. "I'm a man. Men don't carry umbrellas."

"I'm a woman. I carry a big umbrella," she said, tipping her forehead to the umbrella holder by the door. "Mine's the polka-dot one about four-feet high."

"Is that supposed to be a substitute for something, Michele?"

"Oh yes. You've figured me out. I have penis envy, so I carry a large stick." She patted the wooden stool next to her. "Sit. Have a drink."

"I need one," he said, taking off hia jacket and toss-ing it on the back of the stool. "Whiskey. Straight up," he told the bartender.

When the glass of amber liquid arrived, he downed it in one quick swallow then ordered another. That glass earned the same treatment. Michele arched an eyebrow. "Shit day?"

"Shit week," he muttered, running a hand roughly through his hair. He was sure his hair was standing up, unkempt. He'd been pushing his hands through it all week, as if that motion would someone ease the coiled frustration that had taken up residence in his bones and bloodstream, courtesy of one Julia Bell. It made no sense to him. He'd studied it from all angles, turned it inside and out and around. He didn't under-stand how they could have had the time together they did—a weekend that was unforgettable—and then de-scended into radio silence.

"Talk to me," Michele said, placing a gentle hand on his arm. He looked down at her hand. Everything about her was familiar and safe. He'd known her for years, and though he'd never put his hands on her again after that one drunken kiss in college, there was something comforting about her. Maybe because they were long-time friends; maybe because she was a shrink. She helped people for a living. Maybe she could help him make sense of that woman's exodus.

"Fine," he said, because the alcohol had already loosened him up. He wanted to jettison this tangle of anger and hurt from his chest. "You ready for this?"

"The doctor is in session," she said, sitting up straight and proper. "Only for an after-hours session, I insist on another one of these." She tapped his glass.

She ordered another round as he began talking.

"I met someone," he started, then told her the story. Not every detail. He wasn't about to confess that he'd had a raging hard-on for the last week and refused to do anything about it because he knew he'd think of Julia, and he wanted to stop thinking of his fiery red-head. He didn't tell her either that making love to that woman had been the most intense sexual encounter of his life. She was his perfect partner in every way—in the bedroom, and outside the bedroom. He'd never enjoyed a woman's company as much as hers, and he'd felt like they could do anything together. "We had a great time. A perfect weekend. And we were falling for each other. I was sure of it. Talked about seeing each other again, making a go of it," he said and Michele's features tightened; her lips pursed as he told her about the plans they made for a long-distance affair. "Everything seemed like it was clicking on all cylinders. Every single thing."

She drew in a sharp breath. "Every thing?" Her voice sounded strained as if the question were hard for her.

"Yeah," he said, trying to keep the desire out of his voice. His throat was parched just thinking of Julia. "We had a connection."

"Oh. I thought you meant . . ." Michele said, then let her voice trail off as she blushed.

He had meant *that*, but he didn't intend to share details of his sex life with Davis's sister. What a man did behind closed doors, or in a town car, or in a bar in the West Village—he shifted uncomfortably, recalling Julia's stoic orgasm at The Red Line as he worked her over under the bar—was between the man and the woman. Only the woman he wanted had run; she didn't want his business. "But the next morning, she was out of here like a bat out of hell. So tell me, Michele. Tell me, my wise little shrink. What am I missing? Is she secretly craving me and can't figure out how to tell me?" he asked, laying it on the line as he ached for an explanation. "'Cause I fucking miss her, and I want her in my life. Did I miss a cue from her? Fuck something up? Is there something I should be doing?"

Michele didn't answer right away. She reached for her glass and took a long drink. After she set it down, she looked straight at him, her dark-brown eyes both intense and caring. "I'm going to be blunt. I'm going to be direct, and talk to you like I would talk to one of my patients. And here's the thing, Clay," she said, reaching out to place her hand on his thigh. "That's not how a woman behaves when she likes a man."

His shoulders sank and he sighed heavily. "Yeah?"

She nodded. "She's history. I hate to say it, because clearly you have it bad for her, but she ran. Maybe there's something in her life that's tying her down. Maybe she has some deep, dark past. Maybe she's secretly married and really only could manage one weekend with you. But if she truly had a great time and truly was open to dating long-distance like she claimed, then she'd have called you when her flight landed. She'd have texted you. She'd be, I don't know," Michele said, forcing out a laugh, "sending you naughty pictures."

Clay winced, and his dick rose to attention at the thought of a naughty picture of Julia appearing on his home screen. Maybe a shot of her topless, of those full luscious breasts that he longed to lick and kiss and squeeze. Or that ass, so round and sexy, and calling out for a spanking. In his mind, he could hear the sound of his palm smacking her ass, the sharp slap, and the surprised *oh* that would fall from her lips, followed by a moan. She liked spankings. He was pissed that he hadn't had the chance to smack her ass more than once.

He wanted to slam his fist against the bar. "So the lack of naughty shots on my phone is the surest sign that this woman is history," he said through tight lips, barely wanting to acknowledge the cold hard truth Michele was laying out for him.

She flashed him a sympathetic smile. "Yes, Clay. She's history. When a woman wants to be with a man, she makes the effort to see him, to call him, to spend time with him, just as he does with her. She aspires to be honest and upfront. To share her heart. Besides, that's what you deserve," she said, and squeezed his arm.

For a second there it felt as if she lingered on his bicep. But maybe it was the booze making his mind fuzzy. Which reminded him—he needed another drink.

By the time he left, he was pretty damn sure he was buzzed. Walking to the subway stop two blocks away, he changed that assessment as the cabs and cars and lights around him grew fuzzier. He wasn't buzzed. He was drunk. So drunk, he saw no reason why he shouldn't text her as he headed down the steps to the platform, reaching for his phone from his pocket, missing it the first time. He nearly stumbled onto the subway car as his fingers flew across the screen.

I can't stop thinking about you.

He hit send, then cursed himself, wished he could take it back. He was going to get nothing in return from Julia, and that would only make her exit burn more.

When he emerged on Christopher Street, he hoped that maybe the gods of drunk-texting were looking out for him. That perhaps there'd been no signal underground, and he'd be saved from his own stupid desires for her.

But there it was, in his sent messages, mocking his traitorous heart.

CHAPTER FIFTEEN

Julia brushed some sugar crystals along the rim of a martini glass, and handed her signature cocktail to a woman in a standard, boring, black business suit who'd wandered in a few minutes ago rolling a large black case on wheels, the kind that was usually full of pharmaceuticals. Julia guessed she was a sales rep for one of the big drug companies and had been pitching docs all day with little success. Quite simply, the woman looked worn down.

She sighed heavily, resting her chin in her palm. Julia felt for her, without even knowing her woes. Life could be a cruel mistress. Sometimes the days wrung you dry. The nights did too, those lonely nights when all she wanted was a note, a moment, a sweet reminder that she wasn't one woman against the world, tackling everything solo.

"Enjoy," Julia said, sliding the Purple Snow Globe in front of the woman. "I hope it makes the day a little better."

The woman flashed a smile. "You have no idea how much I need this."

"This one is my specialty, but if it doesn't fit the bill, you let me know and I'll mix up something else for you instead."

The woman took her first sip, and her tired eyes lit up. Julia swore a switch had been flipped and they'd gone from muted to bright blue. "This is divine."

She smiled. "I'm glad you like it," she said, and for now, this was enough to make Julia's shit week a bit better. She might not have won her game, she might have lost her man, but at least she could do one thing right: mix a drink, and lift the spirits temporarily of the weary.

She moved to the tap, filling a Pale Ale for a regular customer, a skinny guy who always stopped by after work. She liked him; he'd never once tried to hit on her. He was only here for the drinks.

"The usual," she said, handing him the glass. He doffed an imaginary hat, and took his first swallow. She gathered up tips from other patrons and returned to the register, tucking some bills in the drawer.

"Can I pretty please have your most special, awesomest Diet Coke?"

Julia grinned widely, and turned around to see her favorite person ever: her sister McKenna, decked out in a vintage emerald-green dress with a white petti-coat peeking out from the skirt's hem. On her shoulders she wore a faux white fur cape—one hundred percent pure-retro fashionista. Next to her was her fiancé, Chris, wearing a plaid button-down and jeans, dress-up attire for the most casual California surfer guy that he was. They were the happiest couple she knew, and yet another reason why Julia was never going to burst their bubble of bliss with her troubles. Seeing her sister in love was a singular joy, and she'd go to the ends of the earth to protect McKenna's heart from any more hurt.

"Always for you," Julia said, and leaned across the bar to give her big sister a hug. "And hello handsome," she said to Chris, giving him a peck on the cheek.

"Hey, Julia. How's business tonight?"

"Always good at Cubic Z," she said, beaming and glad for the chance to talk about the bar business. She was proud of her tiny little patch of land in SoMa; yet another reason why she desperately wanted to get out from under Charlie's thumb. She didn't want him to take over this place. The thought of him running his illegal operations from her bar, threatening other patsies with his knife that wasn't dangerous in and of itself, but symbolized all he could do, made her stomach restless. He could turn it to rubble too, leaving her, Kim, and Kim's family high and dry. She poured McKenna a Diet Coke, then asked Chris for his poison.

"Whatever's on tap," he said, and she winced inside at the words. Granted, she'd heard that phrase a few times a night, but it reminded her of Clay, of what he'd said the first night they met here. After she handed Chris his glass, she looked from McKenna to her man and back. "What's up with the fancy attire? You going to a ball or something?"

Chris smiled and shook his head. "Nope, but my network is having some shindig to celebrate our record-high ratings, so this is me dressing up," he said, fingering the collar of his shirt.

"You clean up mighty fine," she said, and once again her mind wandered back to Clay, to how delicious he looked in everything and nothing. She loved his sharp style, his power ties and crisp shirts, the cuffs and how he rolled them up revealing those forearms, so thick and strong.

A sharp pang of longing lodged in her chest. She wasn't only yearning for his arms; she was longing for the whole man, inside and out, from the way he held her to how he talked to her. He'd wanted to know more about her, and she felt one hundred percent the same about him. He fascinated her, with his mix of down and dirty, loving and tender. Though it seemed insane to miss someone she'd only spent a few nights with, she'd never met anyone like him, who captivated her mind and her body.

She shook her head, as if she could shake off thoughts of him. She reached for the tap to pour a beer for another customer.

"Speaking of record ratings," McKenna began in that voice that hinted she had something up her sleeve, "Chris is about to renegotiate his contract, and is looking for a new lawyer, so I was thinking about your guy . . ."

Julia's hand froze on the tap and the beer started to overflow the glass.

Your guy. Oh, how she wanted him to be *her guy*, and all that title allowed—the nights, the days, the moments, the tangling up in each other's arms.

"Oh crap," she said when she realized the liquid had frothed over. Grabbing a towel, she wiped down the side of the glass, cleaned it up and handed it to a customer.

"What do you think about that?" McKenna asked when she returned.

"He's pretty kickass at his job, right?" Chris said, chiming in. "I was talking to my sister the other day, and she said he's worked out all kinds of perks for Davis."

Julia straightened her spine. "I don't have any business dealings with him, but from what I've heard, his clients rave about him."

"Can you do an intro or something?"

"You're the one who introduced me to him," Julia pointed out.

"But that was more casual, something I mentioned to him in passing at the theater. I figured for this, a business intro would be better." Then something flashed in McKenna's eyes. Realization, maybe. Julia had been home from her trip for more than ten days and hadn't said much about it, other than a few texts that it went well, and she was home and busy, busy, busy. She hadn't told her sister that she'd bolted. McKenna leaned across the bar and narrowed her eyes. "Are you still into him?"

She was about to fashion an answer when she heard a customer call out. "Oh, excuse me!" The woman in the suit waggled her fingers.

Julia walked over to her. "How was it?"

The woman tapped the glass. "Never had anything like it. It's amazing."

"I'm so glad you liked it."

"Listen. I have a friend—his name is Glen Mills— whose magazine is running a search for the best cocktail ever," the woman continued. "I'm going to tell him about this."

"That'd be nice of you," she said, though she knew patrons said stuff like this all the time, so she didn't put any stock in it. No more, at least, than simple pride in a job well done.

"What's your name?"

"Julia," she told her, as the woman handed her a twenty.

"Keep the change, Julia."

Then she left, rolling her bag on the way out, only this time her pace was upbeat and energetic. Julia returned to her sister, eager to avoid any more talk of Clay. She didn't need to feel that empty ache for him all evening, especially since she was sure to feel it all night long alone in her bed. She looked at her watch. "Hey, it's about to get crowded here."

"So can you do an intro to Clay?" McKenna asked again, and clearly Julia wasn't going to be able to ignore this request.

She mulled over the question. She'd been trying to steer clear of temptation, locking her phone in a kitchen drawer in the evenings when she felt the desire to text him or call, going for a run in the mornings to try to clear her mind. But neither tactic kept him from occupying the prime corner lot in her brain. She'd been dreaming of him every night. The very mention of his name brought a flush to her skin, and heat between her legs. It had been a while; she hadn't even touched herself since she'd left. If she did, she'd only picture him, and that wouldn't help put him out of her mind.

Maybe, just maybe, a brief email for her sister would satiate this longing inside her, and quench her thirst for him. Sort of like a phased withdrawal. One tiny taste, and then she'd be done.

"I'll take care of it for you," she said, and something inside of her dared to spark. At least she had a reason to reach out to him, and she tried not to get too excited about the prospect of sending him a note, but she couldn't help it—she was excited. "Now, can we talk about something besides business please? Like your wedding? That's what I most want to chat about. I can barely wait another month to see my big sister walking down the aisle."

The two of them beamed, Chris and McKenna matching each other in sheer wattage of their smiles. He dropped a quick kiss on her cheek, and she threw her arms around his neck, and Julia was happy for the way her sister could be free with the man she cared for.

"So we're going to have karaoke, as you know," McKenna said and began rattling off all the details, and though Julia knew most of them already since she was Maid of Honor, she didn't mind hearing them again. Her sister's happiness brought a smile to her face, so she listened as McKenna updated her on all their wedding plans, and she too was counting down the days till the two of them got hitched.

* * *

Later that night, as the crowds wound down she reached for her phone to call when she saw Clay had texted her. Her eyes widened, lighting up with anticipation. With hopeful fingers, she slid open the message.

I can't stop thinking about you.

Her heart thrummed hard against her chest as she savored the words, each one like decadent chocolate. She clutched the phone to her chest, as if that simple act would bring him closer. She walked into the back room, needing a moment alone with his text. She closed the door behind her, leaned against it and stared like a love-struck idiot at the screen again, running her fingertip across his message.

She cycled through her options. She could pretend she never saw it. She could delete it. She could keep on ignoring him. But the very thought of that felt like thorns twisting in her gut. She'd been in a funk since she'd left New York. A real ball of piss. She'd slept badly, she'd been sullen when she went for her morning run, and she could barely focus on the book she'd been reading at bedtime. Her thoughts always careened back to him. A reply might unwind some of the tension knitting its way through her body.

Though she knew the risks, she became convinced with each passing second that answering his message wasn't dangerous. It was simply answering a message. Sometimes a cigar was just a cigar.

The very least she could do was write back.

Would love to know what you're thinking about . . .

Only later did she remember she'd forgotten all about McKenna's request for an introduction. So much the better. Another reason to be back in touch.

By the way, my sister's fiancé wants to talk to you about working together. I'll send you his info. Though I still want to know what you're thinking about.

She paused, her thumbs hovering over her smartphone. Then, she added, just so there'd be no misunderstanding, about her intent—*xoxo.*

CHAPTER SIXTEEN

from: cnichols@gmail.com
to: purplesnowglobe@gmail.com
date: April 16, 7:48 AM
subject: What I'm thinking about . . .

Everything. Your hair. Your ass. Your beautiful
breasts. Your lips. You curled up in my bed. Your attitude. Most of all, why the fuck you left like that.

from: purplesnowglobe@gmail.com
to: cnichols@gmail.com
date: April 16, 11:08 AM
subject: The other thoughts please

Something came up. Can we go back to those other
items instead?

from: cnichols@gmail.com
to:purplesnowglobe@gmail.com
date: April 16, 5:48 PM
subject: Not sure . . .

I don't know. Can we?

from: purplesnowglobe@gmail.com
to: cnichols@gmail.com
date: April 16, 11:48 PM
subject: Be sure . . .

You tell me.

from: cnichols@gmail.com
to: purplesnowglobe@gmail.com
date: April 17, 6:48 AM
subject: Ball. In. Your. Court.

You tell me what you're wearing. You tell me if you can't stop thinking about me. You tell me why you're not here spread across my lap, that beautiful ass calling out for my palm.

from: purplesnowglobe@gmail.com
to: cnichols@gmail.com
date: April 17, 9:48 AM
subject: Served

So you're saying you want to spank me?

from: cnichols@gmail.com
to: purplesnowglobe@gmail.com
date: April 17, 3:48 PM
subject: Hand is ready

You have no idea.

from: purplesnowglobe@gmail.com
to: cnichols@gmail.com
date: April 17, 3:49 PM
subject: Ass is too

Oh, I have an idea. I definitely have an idea. And I would like that very much. I also think you have a thing for my ass.

from: cnichols@gmail.com
to: purplesnowglobe@gmail.com
date: April 17, 11:48 PM
subject: More on that

It's perfection. I want to bite it. Lick it. Smack it. Grip it hard while I fuck you.

from: purplesnowglobe@gmail.com
to: cnichols@gmail.com
date: April 18, 1:01 AM
subject: Which means . . .

So you still want me, I take it?

from: cnichols@gmail.com
to: purplesnowglobe@gmail.com
date: April 18, 7:01 AM
subject: Yes

You know I do. That didn't change.

from: purplesnowglobe@gmail.com
to: cnichols@gmail.com
date: April 18, 11:34 AM
subject: Ditto . . .

I still want you . . .

Clay stared at the computer screen, his fingers hovering over the keys, considering a reply. But damn, those words were mocking him. *I still want you.* How could she say that with the way she'd left? It made no sense, and Michele had spelled it out for him in no uncertain terms that if Julia wanted to play ball, she'd be at the plate, not skipping and frolicking along the foul lines, darting in and out of sight. He pushed away from his keyboard, like an alcoholic trying to step away from the bar. Grabbing a pen and a contract from the pile of papers on his desk, he tossed his phone onto his desk, left his office, and locked the door.

If he stayed within typing distance of either device, he'd surely keep up this volley with her. Because she was as irresistible to him as she'd been that very first night. With his head down the whole way, he headed to a bench outside Central Park and settled onto it, trying his best to dive into the fine print on a licensing deal that the actor Liam Connor needed wrapped up before he opened a new restaurant in New York in a few weeks. Clay didn't usually do restaurant deals, but Liam was a long-time client and had asked him to look over the terms with the other co-owner. Clay shoved his hand through his hair as he studied the fine print, but soon the words he knew backwards and forwards, like *indemnify* and *liability,* were levitating off the page and he could barely put them in context. Reading this was a slow, cruel tease because he couldn't focus on a damn thing.

She weaved in front of him like a damn mirage, tantalizing and teasing him. Whenever he opened or closed his eyes, she was there. Beautiful and beckoning, she lured him in. He could picture her, he could feel the trace of her, touch the outline of her. She'd left her mark on him and he wanted her day after day, night after night.

He swore loudly and looked up. No one noticed his cursing. No one cared. It was New York, and the city spun on its own axis. So he sat and stared at the lunchtime crowds, at a harried doctor rushing by in her scrubs, at a guy in a suit, tugging at his tie while tapping out a message on his phone, at a pair of women in sharp jeans and sweaters, each balancing a cardboard tray of lattes in their hands. A bus trudged by on Fifth Avenue, pulling up to the stop and letting off several passengers who looked equally hurried as they raced to their destinations. Somehow, the chaos of the city soothed the tangled knots in his chest for the moment, and calmed his mind. He took a deep fueling breath, and returned once more to the contract.

A half-hour later, he'd found the one clause that concerned him most, so when he met Liam for lunch he told him about the points he wanted to iron out.

"That's why I keep you around, man," the actor said, flashing his trademark smile that made women swoon and patrons pay top dollar to see his face in lights. "You're going to come see me in *The Usual Suspects,* right?"

"As if I'd miss it," Clay said, and mentally marked the date on his calendar to see the stage adaptation of the hit film.

They spent the rest of the meal talking about Liam's upcoming work, the movies they'd both loved and loathed, and sports, always sports.

When lunch ended, Clay simply hoped he could keep harnessing that focus, and use it to stay on track in his business. He didn't need a repeat. When he returned to his office, refreshed—mostly—from the few hours away from electronic tethers, he clicked on his phone and found another message from the woman who was never far from his mind.

from: purplesnowglobe@gmail.com
to: cnichols@gmail.com
date: April 18, 2:23 PM
subject: On the subject of wanting . . .

So unbelievably much . . . in every single way.

All his control unraveled in a second as his skin heated up, and his heart beat faster, pounding against his chest with the aching want to have her in his arms again. Resistance was futile, so he banged out a reply, saved it in his drafts, and told himself he'd see if he still felt the same way that night. When the workday ended, he went to the gym to pound the punching bag until his shoulders were as sore as they'd ever been.

On the way home, he pulled out his phone, opened his drafts and made a decision.

CHAPTER SEVENTEEN

from: cnichols@gmail.com
to: purplesnowglobe@gmail.com
date: April 18, 5:23 PM
subject: Which brings us back to . . .

So why then? Why did you leave?

from: purplesnowglobe@gmail.com
to: cnichols@gmail.com
date: April 18, 8:48 PM
subject: Truth

I was afraid.

from: cnichols@gmail.com
to:purplesnowglobe@gmail.com
date: April 18, 11:24 PM
subject: Truth is good

Of what?

from:purplesnowglobe@gmail.com
to: cnichols@gmail.com
date: April 19, 2:03 AM
subject: It can be . . .

Of getting close.

from: cnichols@gmail.com
to: purplesnowglobe@gmail.com
date: April 19, 7:48 AM
subject: Re: It can be . . .

Don't be afraid.

from:purplesnowglobe@gmail.com
to: cnichols@gmail.com
date: April 19, 11:19 AM
subject: Re: Re: It can be . . .

But I am.

from: cnichols@gmail.com
to: purplesnowglobe@gmail.com
date: April 19, 5:59 PM
subject: Promise

I won't hurt you.

from: purplesnowglobe@gmail.com
to: cnichols@gmail.com
date: April 19, 10:03 PM
subject: Promises, promises

That's easy to promise. Hard to deliver.

from: cnichols@gmail.com
to: purplesnowglobe@gmail.com
date: April 19, 11:08 PM
subject: Question

Are you going to let the fear control you?

Good question.

Was she going to let Charlie control every aspect of her life? Right now, from his perch at the back table in Mr. Pong's, he stared at her like she was a gnat on the bottom of his shoe, and that was after she'd given him his money. The stack was flimsier than usual, but at least she'd won some.

"Get out of here," Charlie said to her in a cold, calculating voice. "You tire me because you take too long."

"I won for you tonight," she pointed out, but then, what was the point? Charlie was in a nasty mood, and maybe it had to do with her, or maybe it had to do with another one of his pawns underperforming.

"Hardly. This is hardly enough," he said, fanning out the thin stack in her face, smacking her on the nose with the bills. She flinched, surprised that money could wound that much.

As she left the Chinese restaurant, nearly bumping into a man with a well-lined face and sad eyes who stared longingly at the sign for Mr. Pong's, she pondered all the fear in her life. She was afraid of Charlie, of the veiled threats of him hurting her, hurting Kim, and taking more and more of her business until he was satisfied. Though men like him never had their fill, did they? She was scared for her sister, and wanted desperately to protect McKenna's hard-won happiness with Chris. Most of all she was terrified of screwing up. What if she couldn't win the rest of the money? Would she be in Charlie's clutches forever? Time was running out, and she pictured him snapping chains on her forever somehow, so she'd never ever escape from him.

She didn't know what would happen.

All she knew for sure was this fear sucked. This emptiness stung. And the only thing that had felt remotely good and real in her life was opening up to Clay. She'd been living in a cocoon of her own necessary lies for so many months, that the sliver of truths she could share with him was freeing.

from: purplesnowglobe@gmail.com
to: cnichols@gmail.com
date: April 20, 2:02 AM
subject: Good question

I don't know . . . I don't want to be controlled by fear . . . but I can't stop wanting you either.

from: cnichols@gmail.com
to: purplesnowglobe@gmail.com
date: April 20, 7:32 AM
subject: New side of you

Don't stop wanting me. This is the most open I think you've been.

from: purplesnowglobe@gmail.com
to: cnichols@gmail.com
date: April 20, 9:52 AM
subject: Blame it on email

Do you like it?

from: cnichols@gmail.com
to: purplesnowglobe@gmail.com
date: April 20, 3:22 PM
subject: Love it . . .

I like nearly everything about you, except when you run from me.

from: purplesnowglobe@gmail.com
to: cnichols@gmail.com
date: April 20, 11:08 PM
subject: Run the other way?

Would you rather I run to you?

from: cnichols@gmail.com
to: purplesnowglobe@gmail.com
date: April 21, 6:03 AM
subject: Yes I would

I would like you on your knees for that smartass comment.

from: purplesnowglobe@gmail.com
to: cnichols@gmail.com
date: April 21, 9:32 AM
subject: Love that position

I would get on my knees for you. You know that. I would get on my knees and take you in my mouth. Under your desk. While you were in a meeting. I love tasting you. So. Much.

from: cnichols@gmail.com
to: purplesnowglobe@gmail.com
date: April 21, 3:43 PM
subject: You're killing me.

I would be stone-faced and not let on.

from: purplesnowglobe@gmail.com
to: cnichols@gmail.com
date: April 21, 4:04 PM
subject: Relentless

I would do everything I could to break you.

from: cnichols@gmail.com
to: purplesnowglobe@gmail.com
date: April 21, 4:14 PM
subject: I know, believe me, I know

I bet you would. I have excellent control.

from: purplesnowglobe@gmail.com
to: cnichols@gmail.com
date: April 21, 7:17 PM
subject: Shifting gears . . .

That's why you're such a good lawyer. By the way,
I hear you're Chris's attorney now. Thank you for
taking care of him.

from: cnichols@gmail.com
to: purplesnowglobe@gmail.com
date: April 21, 7:43 PM
subject: From blow jobs to business . . .

Thank you for the introduction. I'm gonna make
him an even richer mofo.

from: purplesnowglobe@gmail.com
to: cnichols@gmail.com
date: April 21, 11:23 PM
subject: Cocky, and I like it

I bet you are. I wish I had a reason to be in entertainment and have you be my lawyer.

from: cnichols@gmail.com
to: purplesnowglobe@gmail.com
date: April 22, 5:55 AM
subject: If I were

I'd fight for you, Julia. I'd get you everything you wanted. I'd give you everything you wanted.

from: purplesnowglobe@gmail.com
to: cnichols@gmail.com
date: April 22, 10:09 AM
subject: You would . . .

What about you? What do you want?

from: cnichols@gmail.com
to: purplesnowglobe@gmail.com
date: April 22, 5:12 PM
subject: One word

You.

from: purplesnowglobe@gmail.com
to: cnichols@gmail.com
date: April 22, 8:29 PM
subject: Re: One Word

The same. I want the same.

from: purplesnowglobe@gmail.com
to: cnichols@gmail.com
date: April 23, 11:10 AM
subject: You ok?

Still there?

from: purplesnowglobe@gmail.com
to: cnichols@gmail.com
date: April 23, 3:53 PM
subject: Hi

Hey . . . you've been quiet . . . everything OK?
Don't make me call you :)

from: purplesnowglobe@gmail.com
to: cnichols@gmail.com
date: April 23, 9:01 PM
subject: Should I be worried?

Was it something I said?

from: cnichols@gmail.com
to: purplesnowglobe@gmail.com
date: April 23, 9:40 PM
subject: It was something you said . . .

What are you wearing?

from: purplesnowglobe@gmail.com
to: cnichols@gmail.com
date: April 23, 9:52 PM
subject: Not working tonight so the answer is . . .

Shirt. Stockings. Thong. Heels.

from: cnichols@gmail.com
to: purplesnowglobe@gmail.com
date: April 23, 10:04 PM
subject: Hard . . .

Truth?

from: purplesnowglobe@gmail.com
to: cnichols@gmail.com
date: April 23, 10:15 PM
subject: Full truth.

I swear.

from: cnichols@gmail.com
to: purplesnowglobe@gmail.com
date: April 23, 10:22 PM
subject: Better be

Are you sure?

from: purplesnowglobe@gmail.com
to: cnichols@gmail.com
date: April 23, 10:30 PM
subject: 100%

Yes.

from: cnichols@gmail.com
to: purplesnowglobe@gmail.com
date: April 23, 10:37 PM
subject: This is not a request

Take off the underwear.

from: purplesnowglobe@gmail.com
to: cnichols@gmail.com
date: April 23, 10:40 PM
subject: Your wish is my command

Done.

Julia startled when she heard a loud knock on her door. What the hell? It was eleven o'clock at night. Cold dread rushed through her veins. There could only be one person banging hard at this hour. Charlie, or his men. She took off her heels, padded quietly to the door, and peered through the keyhole.

CHAPTER EIGHTEEN

Her body reacted instantly. Viscerally. Her skin heated up, and she swore she was seeing things. To be sure, she slid the chain, unlocked the latch, and drank in the oh-so-welcome sight of Clay standing in the doorway, unknotting his tie then loosening the top button on his shirt.

She wanted to throw her arms around him. Kiss him hard. Tell him how damn happy she was to see him. She parted her lips to speak, but he was too fast. His hands were on her face, cupping her cheeks, his hot gaze raking over her body from head to toe. "You don't have heels on."

"I took them off when I came to the door."

"Put them on."

She slipped out of his grip, bent down and slid her feet into her four-inch red pumps. She grew taller as she stood and came face to face with the man she couldn't forget about. His whole body was ready to pounce, his muscles hard, the vein in his neck throbbing. His stare was dark and intense, and he radiated sexuality. His eyes roamed her body, prowling over her, turning her molten. His hands were clenched at his sides. He took a step closer and cupped her cheeks once more. Her knees nearly buckled; she and Clay were combustible. She wanted him so much, every solitary cell in her body cried out for him. Her skin was ignited, and her heart beat in overtime. She watched him swallow, then brush a thumb over her lips. She panted from that single small touch, and nibbled on his thumb.

His eyes rolled back in his head as she bit gently into him. She thrilled at his reaction, at the way he breathed out hard.

When he opened his eyes, he stared at her momentarily then crushed her lips in a consuming kiss, one that told her he wanted to devour her. That he was hell-bent on it. When he broke the kiss, she went first, whispering her desperate need. "*Take me,*" she said.

"Turn around."

She bent over her kitchen table, her chest on the metal, her ass in the air where she knew he wanted it, offering herself to him to be claimed. She peered back, watching as he finished unknotting his tie and yanked it off, then unbuttoned his shirt.

Her chest rose and fell as she watched him, heat pooling between her legs with every move he made. He left his shirt open, and she marveled at his chest, at the hard planes and ridges. Her hand had a mind of its own, and she twisted her arm around to try to touch him. He swatted her hand away, and pushed her tight black shirt up her back, exposing more of her skin, then he ran his hands up and down her spine. He dipped his hand between her legs, sliding a finger across her swollen lips.

"Oh," she cried out, her eyes falling closed, and her mouth forming a perfect *O*.

"Have you been touching yourself?" he asked, sounding like a lawyer in a courtroom. She was a willing witness, eager to be cross-examined.

"No," she said, and he rubbed his fingers over her once more, drawing out a needy moan. She rocked her ass back against him. He raised his hand, and her breath caught, knowing what was coming. Her eyes widened as he brought his hand to her cheek, a sharp sting radiating across her rear.

He bent down to brush his soft lips against her flesh, and she whimpered as he soothed out the sting with his tongue. He slipped his hand between her legs again, sending sparks of heat throughout her body. "You haven't touched yourself once since I saw you?"

She shook her head. "No, I swear. I knew I'd only think of you if I did, and it would make me crazy not to have you." He thrust a finger inside her, and she saw stars as he flicked her clit with his thumb. "So you saved it all for me?"

"Yes." She panted.

"Good. Because I'm going to take it all. I want it all."

He took his hand away, raising it again and she quivered, knowing he was going to smack her once more. She craved the sharp sweet mix of pleasure and pain, and this time the smack was followed by his fingers gliding between her legs as he rubbed her where she wanted him most.

"I've haven't touched myself either, Julia," he said as he began unzipping his pants. "You know what that means?"

"What does that mean?" she said as he pushed his briefs down, freeing his enormous erection. Her lips parted at the sight of his cock, thick, hard and throbbing. She wanted him so badly. Wanted all of him. He gripped his cock, stroking himself up and down. She watched, mesmerized, as a low moan escaped her.

"It means I've been rock hard since you left me. I've been walking around New York City at full fucking mast, thinking of you and not doing a damn thing about it for the same reason," he said, dragging the head of his cock against her wet pussy lips. Sweet agony sang in her body as she tried to rock back into him, to draw him into her body, awash with never-ending lust. "I didn't want to think about you because you were all I was thinking about already," he said, as he reached into his pocket for a condom, tore open the wrapper, and rolled it on.

"It was the same for me." She could hear the desperation in her own voice. She needed this so much; not just the physical connection that burned hot between them, but she needed *him*. This man, the way he made her feel inside and out. He'd touched something so deep inside of her, a part she'd kept hidden and well protected. But he was there, working his way around the fortress of her hardened heart, and she wanted all of him. She could not be more grateful that he'd shown up tonight—the first clear evidence that maybe her luck was changing. "I kept thinking about you too. I want you so much."

"I want you too." He bent over her body, laying his chest over her as he rubbed his hard length against her entrance. "And I hated the way you left me."

"I hated it too," she said as she writhed against him, struggling to guide him into her. He gripped her wrists over her head, pinning her on the table.

"*Julia*," he rasped out, grazing his mouth along the column of her throat, eliciting a desperate groan from her. "I have to tell you something."

"Yes?" she asked, breathing hard, her back arching, her body molding to his.

He pulled back to look her in the eyes. His voice was ragged. "I'm crazy about you, but right now I'm going to fuck you like I hate you. I need to fuck you angrily but don't forget this: I'm crazy for you."

She bit her lip, desire coursing through her like a shooting star speeding across the sky. "I'm crazy for you," she murmured, but the last word was swallowed as he thrust into her, filling her in one quick move.

She moaned loudly and closed her eyes, savoring the feeling of his hard, hot length inside her. God, he felt amazing, stretching her. He began to pump, hard, fast, rough. Just like he'd promised. Her breasts were smashed against the kitchen table, and she didn't care that they hurt. She welcomed the hurt. The way every part of her body *felt* him. Her legs shook as he drove into her, her wrists twinged with his rough grip, and her cheek throbbed with how she was pressed hard against the unforgiving metal surface. But with each thrust, she took him in deeper, her heat rising. She grew wetter with every punishing stroke, needing terribly for him to fuck all the stress, all the problems, and all the troubles out of her life right now.

"Harder," she urged, and she was rewarded with a slam.

"Be careful what you wish for," he said roughly against her ear.

"I like it like this. I'm not regretting it."

"Don't ever regret me," he said, his stubbled jaw rubbing against her cheek.

"Never," she said in between pants. She raised her ass higher. "Touch me," she said, and she sounded like she was begging, but she knew he'd like that sound.

"You want me to touch your clit?" he asked as he pounded into her.

"Yes, please."

"Good. I like how you asked nicely for it," he said, letting go of her wrists. He stood behind her now, ramming hard as he held her hip with one hand, the other hand reaching between her legs to rub her clit. The second he made contact, she shrieked in pleasure.

"*Yes.*"

It was all she could say. All she could manage. She shouted *yes* over and over as he pounded into her, taking her body, taking it back for him, claiming her with the hard, rough fucking she wanted. His finger raced across her swollen clit, hitting her at just the right pace, just the right friction until the world spun away, and everything blurred out but the unholy pleasure that rang through her body. Her climax rushed over as she tore past the brink. He was there with her, gripping her hips, plunging deeper, unleashing himself until he collapsed on her.

She breathed out hard, panting as if she'd just run a race. Then his lips were on her neck, kissing her softly, gently, as he mapped her with his mouth.

"I'm so crazy about you," he whispered, and though her body was hot from the coming together of their mouths, her heart flooded with warmth too from his words.

"I feel the same, Clay. Exactly the same," she murmured, turning her head so he could dust her mouth with his lips.

He pulled out, tossed the condom in the trashcan, and returned to her. He lifted her spent body from the table, where she was still splayed out, awash in the aftershocks, and glanced around, quickly finding the door to her one bedroom, then he carried her there. He laid her down on the bed, walked to the bathroom, grabbed some tissues and brought them to her. She cleaned up, and handed them to him to dispose of.

She wondered briefly how he'd found her apartment, but figured a quick Google search had likely revealed her address to him.

When he returned once more he scanned her bedroom, and she wasn't sure if he was going to stay the night here or not. Nerves raced through her, as she wondered what he would do next.

CHAPTER NINETEEN

So this is where she lay at night when she'd sent all those emails. Curled up on her king-size bed, on top of the wine-red covers, half-naked, wearing only her shirt .

At least, that's how he liked to imagine her, and how he liked to look at her.

He'd never been one to think much about a woman's home decor, but something seemed quite fitting about the deep reds, royal purples and gold colors in her bedroom—sexy shades for a woman who exuded sexiness in her style.

On her nightstand was an e-reader and he was willing to bet it was well stocked with the books she loved—adventure tales, she'd told him the night they met. Stories of naval rescues at sea, of daring treks up mountains, of beating the odds. She was an adventuresome woman, and what she read reflected that side of her. A purple scarf was draped over the lamp on the nightstand, and his mind flashed to other uses for that scarf. He checked out the framed photos on her bureau—pictures of her sister and her, and her sister and a dog, too.

"That's McKenna's dog. Ms. Pac-Man."

"Cute dog."

"She is cute and smart," Julia said, a note of pride in her voice, almost like an aunt beaming about a child. "She's also loyal and devoted."

"As a dog should be."

"And a person," she added.

"Yes," he said, agreeing emphatically. "Are you loyal and devoted?"

She nodded, her face serious, her green eyes holding his gaze. There was a fierceness in her look. A certainty. "I only want you. I only think of you," she said.

"I know the feeling well."

She patted her bed. "I like the way you look in my apartment."

"I like the way you look right now," he said, climbing up on her bed and joining her.

"Are you going to take off those pants and stay the night?" she asked, eyeing his half-dressed state.

"I am considering it," he said in a wry tone.

"What can I do to convince you?"

He was surprised to find her voice stripped bare of flirting as she posed the question. He was used to her seductive side, the way she'd trail her fingernails along his arm to get what she wanted. But this was a newer side of Julia, a vulnerable one, and it gave him hope that she was finally opening up to him.

He ran his index finger along her jawline. He swallowed, taking a beat. He was going to put it out there. Put himself out there. "Let me in," he said, as he moved his fingers to her heart, tracing it.

"How?" she asked in a wobbly voice.

"Tell me why you're scared. Tell me why you ran."

She sighed heavily, shifting from her side to her back. She closed her eyes; her face seemed pinched. He ran his hand along her bare arm. "Hey," he said softly. "You're here now. I'm here now. I want to know what I need to do so I don't scare you away."

She opened her eyes, turned back to face him. Her expression was softer now. "It's nothing you can or can't do. It's me."

"Right. It generally is. But tell me how I can help you be comfortable with you and me," he said. "Because for a while there I was damn sure you were history. My friend Michele even said so, in no uncertain terms."

Like she'd been burned, Julia jerked away from him, sitting up straight. "Michele? Who's Michele? Your ex?"

He laughed. "Michele is just a friend. Davis's sister. Known her for years. She also happens to be a shrink."

"You were talking to her about me?" Julia crossed her arms.

"Yes," he said, tugging on her hips, trying to pull her back to lie next to him. But she scooted further away into the jumble of pillows by her headboard. "Hey, I was talking to her about you because I like you, woman. Get that straight."

She narrowed her eyes, fixed him with a harsh stare, but said nothing.

"And I was trying to understand you, and I still don't entirely understand, so help a man out."

"Fine, but I don't want other women touching you," she said sharply as she glared at him.

Another laugh took hold of him, deep and rumbling through his chest. It warmed him up, knowing how possessive she was. "I believe I've made it patently clear that I am a one-woman kind of man, and you are my kind of woman. But this conversation isn't about me. I want to know what's going on with you," he said, succeeding this time in tugging her alongside him.

She took a breath, pursed her lips together, and then exhaled. She looked him square in the eyes; her pretty greens were tinged with sadness and a trace of fear. His heart lurched towards her, wanting to help her, reassure her. She licked her lips, and spoke in a wobbly voice that grew stronger as she pushed through. "I've got some trouble from my past chasing me. And I can't say anything more, because I don't want you or anyone I care about to get caught up in my problems."

He started to speak, to tell her he wasn't afraid of problems, and he certainly didn't expect anyone to come to a relationship baggage-free, but she held up her hand to silence him.

"Eventually, I'll be free of it, but right now there's just stuff I have to deal with, and that's why I left so quickly," she said, her voice raw and pained. "I'm sorry."

"Is somebody hurting you?" he asked, clenching his fists as he kept his voice on an even keel. He didn't want to scare her, but he sure as hell would hurt anyone who laid a hand on her.

"No," she said quickly, shaking her head. "Nor do I have a pill problem, or anything like your ex, I swear." She gripped his bicep, digging her fingers into his flesh to make her point. "I promise."

"That is excellent news. But what sort of trouble is it, then?"

"Clay," she said, soft, but insistent in her tone. "That's all I want to say. I have to keep the people I care about out of it. And I care about you. So deeply, and more than I ever thought I would," she said, reaching for his hand, and threading her soft fingers through his. "So much more," she added, squeezing his hand for emphasis, and her touch sent a shiver through him. She kissed his hand. By God, he could get used to this side of her. He would love to see this part of her every day. "It's my problem to deal with, and I'm dealing with it."

He wanted to help her, but he wasn't sure she'd let him so he tried another way to understand the scope of this *problem.* "Is it something I should be worried about?"

She shook her head. "No."

He raised an eyebrow, studying her face, trying to read her. He wasn't sure what was going on, but something in his gut said she was telling the truth. Or maybe he just wanted to believe her. Maybe he *could.* For now, at least. "Okay, I will try my best not to worry for now then," he said, though he knew that would be a tall order because already—deep in his gut —he was concerned for her, for everything about her. He wanted to protect her, look out for her. That she was hardly the kind of woman who needed taking care of didn't factor into his thinking one bit. She was his, and he couldn't abide by anyone hurting her.

"Good," she said, and her face lit up again, her mischievous grin reappearing as she danced her fingers down his chest. "So, to what do I owe the pleasure of this surprise late-night visit?"

"In town for a meeting. I'm seeing Chris tomorrow about his renegotiations."

"McKenna didn't mention it to me."

He tapped her nose. "It was last-minute. Just scheduled it today, and caught an evening flight. I'm heading to L.A. early afternoon, so I'm squeezing the meeting in beforehand."

"I am glad you squeezed me in," she said, her hand darting to the waistband of his pants. "Now, have I successfully convinced you to take these off and spend the night with me? I'm not much of a cook, but I do know where I can take you tomorrow morning for some fantastic pancakes."

He pretended to think deeply about the food. "I do love pancakes."

"And spending the night with me. You better love that too," she said, playfully swatting him.

"I believe I could find it in me to enjoy another night with you."

"Wait. Where's your bag?"

"In the town car. Driver's waiting outside."

"So you could make a getaway?"

He shook his head. "Gorgeous, when is it going to get through to you that I'm not the one who's running? Nor am I a presumptuous asshole who's going to show up at your doorstep with an overnight bag unless you want me to."

"I want you to," she said in a sexy purr.

He dialed his driver, and a minute later, there was a knock on the door. Clay retrieved his bag, tipped the driver and said goodnight. He returned to Julia's room to find her leaning against the wall, her shirt shucked off and her stockings removed, wearing only her red pumps. Her hips jutted out seductively and his dick rose to full attention as he drank in the sight of her, the moonlight casting midnight blue shadows across her long and lean body, highlighting her curves.

"You didn't think I was going to bed, did you?"

"Not for a second."

"I want to show you one of my favorite positions."

"I have a feeling it's going to be one of my favorite positions too," he said as he kicked off his pants, and placed them on a chocolate-brown chair in the corner of her bedroom.

She pointed to the bed. "Take off the briefs, and sit down."

"At your service," he said, stripping off his final layer, and parking himself on the edge of her bed. She looked him over from head to toe, and he wasn't going to deny it—the hunger in her eyes was the biggest turn-on of his life. She stared at him like she'd never wanted anyone so much. As if she had never laid eyes on a man she wanted to feast on like this. Tremors rolled through him, and he ached with desire for her.

A low growl took hold in his chest as she strutted over to him. The sight of her gorgeous body was something he'd never get enough of. She stopped, placing her hands on his shoulders, leaning into him so her breasts brushed his face. A bolt of heat tore through him, and he reached for her, craving closeness, needing her beautiful body pressed against his. But she pulled back, wagging her finger, then walked away, heading for her nightstand. She grabbed the purple scarf and returned.

"What's good for the goose is good for the gander," she said in that sexy, smoky voice that could lead him to say yes to anything she wanted.

"You tying me up?"

"Just a little bit," she said, as she straddled him, sitting across his thighs. He felt the heat from her pussy even though she wasn't close to touching his cock. Still, being near his favorite place made his dick throb. She pressed against him once more, reaching her arms around him. She tugged at his hands on the mattress, adjusting them behind his back. She wrapped the scarf around his wrists, tying them together.

"Hey Julia, I got a question for you," he said as she tugged on the ends of the scarf.

"I grant you permission to ask."

He chuckled. "I haven't been with anyone in several months and I'm clean. How about you? Any chance you're on birth control?"

She leaned back, looked him in the eyes. "I am indeed. You saying you want to feel me coming on your cock in just a few minutes?"

He narrowed his eyes, and growled a hot *yes*.

"Then you can come and play without a glove," she said, gripping his cock in her fist. His hips nearly shot off the bed at her touch. Anything she did to him sent shocks of pleasure through his bones.

"I can not wait to feel your hot pussy surrounding me."

"You won't have to wait much longer, because I'm wet for you," she said, dropping her free hand between her legs and stroking herself.

His chest tightened and his dick throbbed in her hand. He watched her hungrily as she coated her fingers in her own wetness, then brought her finger to his lips.

"Rub yourself on me," he instructed her.

"As you wish." She traced his mouth and he licked his lips, drinking up the taste of her.

"More," he said, and his blood flowed thick and heavy as she slipped her fingers inside her pussy, drawing out more of her delicious juices. She dragged her fingers against him once more, and this time he sucked on her index finger, drawing it all the way into his mouth, lapping up every delicious ounce of her desire. "You taste fucking spectacular."

"Oh I do, do I?" she said seductively, brushing her breasts against his chest.

"You do, Julia. I love your taste, and your smell, and right now you smell like you want me inside you."

"I want to ride you so bad," she said, and swiveled around, straddling him again, only this time her back was to him.

"You are a cruel woman. You know I want to touch your breasts right now."

"And squeeze them too," she added, as she positioned herself over him, rubbing the head of his cock between her legs. Heat seared in his body, like flames licking across his skin. She leaned her head back, her gorgeous red hair fanning out across his chest and his shoulders, taunting him. He craved the chance to grip it hard, and tug, and she knew it. As she rubbed her wetness over him, she licked his neck up to his ear, driving him mad with desire. "Ask for it," she purred.

"Fuck me please," he said, his breath jagged as lust poured through every inch of his body.

She sank down on him, and he groaned loudly. The feel of her hot pussy gripping him tight was like a fevered dream. But it was real, everything real and raw and lingeringly primal in the way she rode him, taking her time, rising up and down on his cock, riding him like he was her plaything, and he wanted nothing more than to be just that in this moment.

His hands itched to touch her, to grab her hips, to hold on hard to her beautiful breasts. But he knew she was the kind of woman who let herself be dominated, but in return, sometimes she needed to take the reins. He let her have all the control, enjoying the view of her perfect body moving up and down on him as her moans grew louder, and more erratic until she was shouting his name, and the feel of her coming undone on his cock was all he needed to join her in climax.

* * *

The hot water beat down on his head and he soaped up Julia's breasts. For the twentieth time.

Though it might have been the thirtieth, or fortieth. It was hard to count. They were too hard to resist.

"Hey, Mister. I'm pretty sure my breasts are scrub-a-dub clean. There's not an ounce of dirt on them," she said, poking his chest.

"Mmm . . . let me just make sure," he said, lathering them up once more. "You might be able to hypnotize me with these breasts."

"You will do my bidding," she said as she swayed her chest in a mesmerizing rhythm, then her hand quickly darted up and she snagged the soap from him. "Ha!" She held it up victoriously. "Now, I can finally get clean, because this gal wants to go to sleep."

He grabbed the soap back from her, tugged her sexy body against his. "Let me. I promise to wash the rest of you."

"Fine," she said, holding out her hands. "Have at me."

He kneeled down in the shower, the water pelting his back as he washed her legs, then gently between her legs, then back up to her belly and down her arms. He rubbed the soap once more against his palms, then dropped it in the soap dish and washed her neck. She leaned her head back, exposing the delicious column of her throat to him. Tenderly, he ran his hands over her, then positioned her under the water and rinsed her off. He wrapped his arms around her, her trim waist fitting perfectly in his embrace.

"Mmm. I like holding you," he whispered, as he closed his eyes.

He could feel her smiling as she molded her body against his, taking what he was giving her. "I know," she said in a soft, sleepy voice. "I like being held by you, Clay. And I'm so glad you're here tonight."

It was the *so* that took hold in his heart, finding purchase, tethering him to her. He thought he could deny himself. He almost believed he could forget her. But he was too far gone to let her go. She was his, and there were simply no two ways about it. She had to be in his life. "Me too."

Soon, she broke the embrace, and took her turn washing him, working her nimble hands across his body, the mischievous look in her eyes telling him that she enjoyed touching him as much as he craved her touch. She stopped at his arm, running a finger along the lines of his tattooed bicep. "Passion," she said, in a reflective voice. "This is so you. It's perfect for you. You are the most passionate man I have ever known. You are passionate in your heart, and passionate in bed, and passionate in your beliefs, and in every single thing you do."

She *got* him. She knew him. She understood who he was, and what made him tick. It was heady being that connected to someone. "It's easy to be passionate with you, Julia."

"And thank you for letting me do that just now in the shower," she said, trailing her fingers across his shoulder.

"For washing me?" He arched an eyebrow in question.

She nodded. "And for letting me tie your hands."

"As I've said before, I've got no issues. No hang-ups. I'm pretty much game for anything and good to go."

"I like that."

"What about you? Anything you don't want me to do?" He asked as she turned the shower off and handed him one of her big fluffy towels, taking another one for herself. "Nice towel," he mentioned offhand.

She didn't answer immediately; instead she folded her towel in half, then in quarters, the long way. He watched her curiously. She raised the towel to her eyes. A knowing grin broke across his face for having gotten her charade.

"Got it. No blindfolding."

She returned to drying off. "I just like to be able to see, that's all. Blindfolding is the only thing that I'm not wild about. And it's not because I have some terrible past with trauma about blindfolding. But the thought of it makes me feel a bit too vulnerable, and for a woman with trust issues, well, I'm not sure it's the best kind of kink for me."

She hung up her towel on a hook and he did the same.

"There are many other forms of kink that I'm happy to try with you, Julia," he said, then reached for her hand and led her back to her bedroom. Once they slipped under the covers, he wrapped his arms around her, then brushed her hair away from her ear. "I guess I'll just have to imagine then how you'd look with my tie over your eyes, wearing nothing but stockings, sitting in a chair and touching yourself while I watch."

She craned her neck to give him a curious stare. "Is that your fantasy?"

He nodded. "It is one of many."

"Maybe someday, handsome. Maybe someday."

"I have another fantasy," he murmured softly in her ear, tugging her closer as they spooned.

"What's that?" she asked.

"Falling asleep with you in my arms."

"I think that's about to become your reality."

"Lucky me."

CHAPTER TWENTY

The pancakes were as delicious as she'd promised. With breakfast finished, they walked past a block full of graffiti art and consignment shops in the Mission district. An up-and-coming neighborhood full of hipsters and Internet startup folks, the shops here bore the evidence of the clientele, but there was an element to these few blocks that bothered him. He didn't like the idea of her living in a neighborhood still plagued with crime and trouble, even if the numbers were improving. She was an independent woman though, and it wasn't his place to criticize where she lived.

"You like living here?" he asked, keeping the question casual.

"Sure," she said with a laidback shrug as they sidestepped a sleeping homeless man. "There's a kick-ass bakery a few blocks over, some fabulous coffee shops, and lots of boutiques that my sister loves, so I get to see her more often."

"Maybe we should all do something next time I'm in town," he suggested, and couldn't deny the touch of nerves in his chest. Last time he'd asked for something more, she'd gone running. But maybe dinner with her sister was something she could handle.

"I would love that," she said, and his nerves departed with her simple answer. "And you're going to love Chris. He's the best."

"I'm looking forward to meeting him in person," he said, checking the time on his watch, "in about twenty minutes."

"Let's get your bag so you're not late," she said as they turned onto her block, passing a vintage clothing shop a few doors down. His driver waited in a town car by her building. Clay gave him a quick wave, then headed to her third-floor apartment. Her cell phone was still on the kitchen counter. She'd left it there all morning, and he'd been grateful to have her undivided attention, a luxury he'd rarely had with Sabrina. He grabbed his suitcase and tapped her metal table. "Good table. That's a keeper."

"I was planning on framing that table because I love what we did on it so much," she said, and then led him back down the stairs and out of her building.

She stopped in her tracks and cursed under her breath. "Fuck," she muttered, and ran a hand through her hair.

"What is it?" he asked, and his shoulders tightened with worry. He zeroed in on her eyes then followed her line of sight to a large man built like a slab of meat pacing a few feet away. The man had black hair, with a white streak down the side. He was scanning the street, and very quickly set his eyes on Julia.

Instantly, Clay reached for her, draping an arm protectively around her. He turned to look at her, holding her gaze tight with his own. "You okay?"

"Yeah," she said in a thin voice as the freight-train-sized man walked toward them.

"You know him?"

"Sort of," she said, as she pressed the tip of her tongue nervously along her teeth.

"Julia," the man barked as he reached them. "You don't answer your phone? Is everything okay?" He sounded strangely concerned, almost paternal, and that irked Clay.

"I was out to breakfast," she said through tight lips. Clay glanced from Julia to the man and back, wanting to know who the hell he was and why he was talking to her like he owned her.

"Charlie needs you tonight."

Julia didn't answer him.

"Julia," Clay asked carefully. "Who's this?"

The man held out a hand, flashed a toothy smile. "I'm Stevie. Who are you?"

Before he could answer, Julia squeezed his arm tightly, some kind of signal, it seemed, then started talking. "This is Carl. Carl and I met last night at the bar. He's just heading home now."

She shot Clay a pleading looking, asking with her eyes to go along with the lie.

"Nice to meet you, Carl," he said, and out of the corner of his eye, Clay noticed a bulge by the man's shins, as if a hard, square barrel of a gun were held safely in place with an ankle holster. Clay didn't have a clue who this man was or why he was packing, but blood rushed fast through his veins, adrenaline kicking in as he quickly cycled through escape routes for the two of them if he pulled it. Down the block, into the building, behind the car. Or better yet, Clay could move first if he needed to. He could take this man; Stevie was big and slow, and Clay had speed on his side. A quick, hard jab to the ribs would double him over, giving them time to get away.

"Likewise," Clay said, calling on his best acting ability. He had no idea why she needed him to lie, and he didn't like it one bit, but he wasn't going to make things worse for her in the moment. Papa bear attitude or not, the man had *thug* or *dealer* written all over him.

Dealer.

Once that notion touched down in his head, he couldn't unsee it or unhear it. It was déjà vu all over again. The sidewalk felt shaky, and the stores on the other side of the street seemed to fall in and out of focus. His chest tightened, and his heart turned cold as if she'd just shoved him into a walk-in freezer.

"When you don't answer," the man said, tilting his head, and explaining in a gentle voice that didn't match his size or his weaponry, "Charlie gets worried."

"I'll be there," she said, and her voice was strained, her body visibly wracked with fear

The man nodded, seeming satisfied with her answer. "I will tell him. See you later. And nice meeting you, Carl."

He walked away, his big frame fading down the block. Clay turned to her. "What was that about? Why did you tell him we met at the bar last night?"

Something dark and sad clouded her eyes. "I don't want him to know who you really are."

"What the hell, Julia?" he asked, his heart still thumping fast and furious. He took a deep fueling breath. "He. Had. A. Gun."

"I know," she said in a broken whisper, a guilty look in her eyes.

"What kind of mess are you in?" he said, holding his hands out wide.

"I can't tell you. You just have to trust me on this. I couldn't say anything about you or use your real name or anything."

"Because?" he asked, annoyed as hell now because she was giving him no reason to think this was acceptable. Lies were never acceptable.

"Just because."

"Who are these people, Julia? Why does Charlie need you tonight, and why does Stevie carry a concealed weapon?" He wished he were in a courtroom because he usually knew the answers to the questions he asked. Now he was swimming blind, without a clue as to his direction.

"There's something I have to help Charlie with," she said, and it was one of the most dissatisfying answers he'd ever heard, and it left an acrid taste in his mouth. He was ready, so damn ready to get the hell out of town. A knot of anger rolled through him, but then he swallowed it away, because there was that image burned in his brain—the outline of a gun. And if you weren't the one carrying the gun, you were usually the target. Julia was in danger, and he couldn't abide by that.

His feelings for her ran too deep to just walk away.

He needed to do everything he could to get her out of the line of fire. He softened, cupping her shoulders. "If you're in trouble, let me help you," he offered, doing his best to let go of his past with Sabrina and to trust the woman in front of him, especially after last night and how she'd seemed to finally open up. "If there's something going on, I want to help you. I know my way around."

"I can't. I have to do this on my own."

"Why?" he asked, the word strangled in his throat.

"You have to trust me on this."

"You're making it awfully hard to trust you," he said, tucking a strand of hair behind her ear.

Her lower lip quivered. "I know," she said, and her voice was starting to break.

"Tell me," he said, pleading now. "Tell me what is going on. Tell me what they want from you. What they have on you. I'm a goddamn lawyer, Julia."

"Clay," she said, softly, pushing back. "You negotiate deals for actors and directors."

He exhaled sharply, not liking the way she'd put that. "Yes, that's what I do, and I'm damn good at it. That means I know how to solve problems, and I also understand the fine nuances of how people interact, and when you— " He stopped talking to point at her "—lie to someone who's carrying a gun, that's a problem. And I want to help solve that problem, if you'll let me."

She worried away at her lower lip, and he wanted to gently kiss her fears away and tell her it would all be fine. But he had no way of knowing that, because she'd given him no reason to put faith in her words.

"I appreciate that. You have no idea how much. But I can't let you do it."

"Can you give me a reason why? Because every instinct inside of me is telling me to walk away and not look back. You told me last night not to worry, and now I am worried, because whatever trouble you're in is looking bigger and bigger. So why won't you let me help you?"

She squeezed her eyes shut, so tight and hard as if she were in pain. Then she opened them, and it was like looking in a mirror—her eyes were etched with the same kind of desperation he felt. The problem was, she held all the cards, and he didn't even know what game they were playing.

"I just need you to trust me. That's all. I need you to. I swear I need you to."

He ran his fingers gently through her hair, wanting, wishing to be able to do this with her. To go all in. But the moment was far too familiar, and it felt like a flashback to his worst times, especially when she grabbed his arm hard. "Please," she said.

He'd been here; he'd seen the same routine from Sabrina, begging him to believe her, pleading with him to see that she wasn't hopped up on pills. Claiming she was getting help, when she was really selling off her purses and jewelry to buy more drugs. He has no idea if Julia was buying drugs, or shaking off a past as a stripper, or hiding some other dark secret, because she wouldn't say. She wouldn't give him the courtesy of the truth. That left him with one cold, hard fact—she was lying. Whether directly or by omission didn't matter. She wasn't being honest.

And that both hurt and pissed him off.

His veins felt scrubbed raw with a scouring pad as he gently, but firmly, peeled her hand off his arm. He didn't need this in his life again. He had business to take care of for his clients, and he couldn't risk the chance of another fucked-up relationship with a trouble-laden woman distracting him from his job.

Julia was perfect and captivating, clever and sexy, and tattooed head-to-toe with the warning sign that read *trouble ahead*. Good thing he'd seen it now before he went in too deep.

"I can't do this Julia," he said, grabbing the handle of his suitcase. "I need to go."

He shut the car door hard behind him, locking it, as if that would keep thoughts of her at bay. He couldn't risk letting a deal slip through his fingers again, and certainly not over a woman messing with his head, and his heart. There was one choice for him now.

He'd have to find a way to forget her, hard and fast.

* * *

She dug her heels into the ground, imagining weights pinning her down, preventing her from doing what she desperately wanted to do.

Go after him.

She bit down hard on her bottom lip. Something, anything so she wouldn't shout his name, chase the car down the street, bang her fists on the metal, and beg him to roll down the window so she could tell him that she wasn't lying; she was protecting him.

But she couldn't live with the chance that he'd become a target too.

She wanted him in her life, wanted him with every ounce of her being. But seeing him hurt would be worse. She sank down on the cold concrete steps of her building, crumpled in a mess. Like her whole damn life, and her stupid heart too. A heart that ached for the man she'd fallen hard for, and had to let go.

Stay tuned for the conclusion of Julia and Clay's love story in AFTER THIS NIGHT releasing May 12...

Check out my contemporary romance novels!

Caught Up In Us, a New York Times and
USA Today Bestseller! (Kat and Bryan's romance!)

Pretending He's Mine, a Barnes & Noble and
iBooks Bestseller! (Reeve & Sutton's romance)

Trophy Husband, a New York Times and
USA Today Bestseller! (Chris & McKenna's romance)

Playing With Her Heart, a USA Today
Bestseller! (Davis and Jill's romance)

Far Too Tempting, an Amazon romance
bestseller! (Matthew and Jane's romance)

And my USA Today Bestselling
No Regrets series that includes

The Thrill of It
(Meet Harley and Trey)

and its sequel

Every Second With You!

ACKNOWLEDGMENTS

The first and most important thank you goes to *you*. The reader. The person holding an eReader in her hands. I hope you enjoyed this story. I loved writing it, and I love being a part of this indie romance world because of the direct connection to readers. So thank you from the bottom of my heart for picking up a copy of Night After Night. You are the reason I write.

I am also immensely grateful to Cara, Hetty and Kim who encouraged me to write this story. Actually, they did more than encourage. They pretty much insisted. They kind of handcuffed me and shook me down and said 'GIVE US MORE CLAY NOW.' Then they uncuffed me, and I immediately set to writing, and boy, am I glad I did. Because Julia and Clay were so much fun to write.

A big thanks to my early readers including Cara, who gives good beta, and Kim Bias, who has an eagle eye and always knows the final touches that my books need. Kim – you have become indispensable to me! A big thanks to Zoe for her faithful reads, and to Kelley, who suggested some important tweaks. My editor Lauren McKellar is my final line of defense and I am grateful for her red pen. And my other Kim – thank you for all those tips. Wink, wink.

Then there is Jen McCoy. This girl. What can I say? Not much that's appropriate, but she is the bomb and I am soooo glad we are friends, and that you'll be there for me to clear my browser history if I ever need you.

Sarah Hansen, once again, designed a gorgeous cover. My jaw dropped when I saw the cover for this book as well as First Night. She is a wizard and an artist and I am a lucky writer that I convinced her to do so many of my covers.

Kelly and Kelley get me through every day and every book. Kelly, my publicist, is my strategist, cheerleader, advocate and true partner-in-crime, and Kelley keeps the whole operation ticking. Helen Williams designs amazing graphics and makes me laugh.

A huge shoutout to my girls - Melody, Kendall, Violet, Monica, Jessie, Lexi and Sawyer. You have become a true circle of friends, and we work hard and play hard in the NWB!

I am so thrilled to give a special nod of thanks and love to the gals who rock the apple world! You are a passionate, dedicated, amazing group of ladies and I'm talking about Naomi Elliott, Courtney Whaley, Lindsay Errington, Joyce Taibleson, Kimberly Mathon, Maria Poli, Kirstyn Renee Walters, Anna Caron, Jen Haldane, Debbie, Heidi B, Keisha Jamison-Mitchell, C. Ebels, Jen Rubio, Blia Hoopes, Yesenya Sanchez and Angelica Maria Quintero Becerra.

Thank you to early readers like Lara, Tiffany, Tiffany, Jennifer, Jamie, Reneall and Ginny for loving Clay.

Big thanks and love to many amazing supporters including: Lexi from Book Reviews by Lexi, Jennifer Santoro, Darcey Smith, Kelley, Kristyn and Tracey from Smut Book Junkie Book Reviews, Jennifer Marr, Kenna Nauenburg, MJ Fryer, Tanya at After the Final Chapters, Jennifer from Jen's Book Reviews, Tabby at Insightful Minds, Kristy Louise, Kara and Sandra from Two Book Pushers, Hetty from BestSellers & BestStellars, Jacquie Lamica, Tee From Kaidans Seduction, Yvette and Michelle from Nose Stuck in a Book, Vanessa Foxford, Valencia from Trulee V's Spot, Kim Bias, Sara Howe, Brenda Howe, Retta Rusaw at Because I Said So, Patricia Lee from A Literary Perusal, Theresa Potter, Stacy Hahn, Jassie DC, Julie Jules, Gretchen from About That Story, Tori from Give Me Books, Karen at The Danish Bookaholic, Crystal Perkins, Betsy from Book Drunk Blog, Tami Jo Schafer , Jennifer's Taking a Break, Simply Kristen, Helen from All Booked Out, Tink Bell, and Jaime Collins-Milo at For the Love of Books by Jaime.

Finally, massive hugs and love to my husband and my children. Somehow, they continue to put up with my daydreaming and drifting off to a fictional world that feels so real to me.

By my side every day as I write are my faithful dogs. I could not imagine writing without their company. Love you mutts! Dogs rule.

CONTACT

I love hearing from readers! You can find me on Twitter at twitter.com/laurenblakely3, or Facebook at facebook.com/LaurenBlakelyBooks, or online at Lauren Blakely.com. You can also email me at laurenblakelybooks@gmail.com.

32248197R00161

Made in the USA
Lexington, KY
14 May 2014